W9-CZO-888

STERLING NORTH
NORTH
THE
WOLFLING

A DOCUMENTARY NOVEL OF THE
EIGHTEEN-SEVENTIES
ILLUSTRATED BY JOHN SCHOENHERR

*This low-priced Bantam Book
has been completely reset in a type face
designed for easy reading, and was printed
from new plates. It contains the complete
text of the original hard-cover edition.*
NOT ONE WORD HAS BEEN OMITTED.

RL 5, IL 6

THE WOLFLING

*A Bantam Book / published by arrangement with
E. P. Dutton & Co., Inc.*

PRINTING HISTORY

A portion of this novel first appeared in AUDUBON MAGAZINE,
July 1969

Dutton edition published August 1969
2nd printing .... August 1969   3rd printing .. November 1969
Family Bookshelf edition published August 1969
Book-of-the-Month Club edition published January 1970
Science Book Club edition published March 1970

Bantam edition / November 1970
2nd printing ... December 1971
Bantam Pathfinder edition / August 1973
4th printing .... July 1974
Bantam edition / May 1976
6th printing ... September 1978

ISBN 0-553-12587-7

Published simultaneously in the United States and Canada

PRINTED IN THE UNITED STATES OF AMERICA

To my father
DAVID WILLARD NORTH
(1862–1962)
whose spirit still pervades
the marshes and woodlands
of southern Wisconsin

Contents

One Hundred Years Ago

(More or Less)

Almost every century is a very good century to be alive —if you are young. One hundred years ago in Wisconsin, there were great flocks of wild geese, ducks and passenger pigeons. The streams were clear and full of fish. Just over the western horizon lay the alluring frontier.

But every century also has its problems not so unlike those we have today. The country had just endured the bloody and divisive Civil War. America's most beloved president, Abraham Lincoln, had been murdered by a crazed assassin. Then, after years of inflation, came the Panic of 1873.

From my father's voluminous letters about his boyhood and from my own knowledge of this beautiful region, I have tried to re-create the life of southern Wisconsin one hundred years ago.

I hope this narrative brings to life some of the characters of that era, particularly Thure Kumlien, the great Swedish-American naturalist, who taught my father to know all the birds and beasts, flowers and trees of the entire area.*

In a sense this is a documentary novel, as authentic as I can possibly make it. But in another sense it is a parable of life yesterday, today and tomorrow. We have only one life to live. Let us hope that we all live it meaningfully.

STERLING NORTH
Morristown, New Jersey

* Please see the documentary notes at the back of the book.

1: The Stile Between Two Worlds

"Awa—oooh—ooh, awa oooooooooo!" The lonesome howl, like the wail of a lost spirit, came eerily from the deep woods to the east where the sun had only begun to tint the snowy horizon. Robbie Trent, who always said he was "not afeared of wolves," shivered deliciously under the homespun counterpane and snuggled down in the feather bed that topped the cornhusk mattress. Little drifts of new snow had filtered in through the hand-split shakes that roughly shingled the cabin roof. The world outside had a fresh white cover, to hide the stained drifts of February.

"Awa . . . OOOOH . . . OOOH!" There it came again, louder and nearer, sending ice water along the boy's spine. It was good to be lying here, safe in the loft, listening to the wild cry. This was the first wolf he had heard in many months. Traps and poison had almost exterminated these swift-moving hunters from the forests of southern Wisconsin. Supposing the time came when there were no more timber wolves, when the last shaggy beast had been slaughtered, the last wolfling dug from the den and clubbed to death by the wolfers! No longer would the thrilling, spine-tingling howl of these great dogs of the wilderness echo across the valley of Lake Koshkonong. It made Robbie very sad to think of a world so bereft.

Robbie rose early, gulped his breakfast, hurried through the chores and was soon on the path to Busseyville. Each Saturday he made this joyful trip, ostensibly to bring the mail, but also to see where the grouse were bedding, what animals had left their tracks upon the snow, and whether the raccoons had yet come forth from their hollow trees. With Old Tessie at his heels he started across the wintry field, his anticipation mounting as he approached the eastern margin of his father's acreage. He was beginning to realize that the zigzag fence between the Trent farm and the Kumlien property was the boundary between two contrasting worlds.

On the Trent side, on land that had once been prairie, corn shocks stood in neat rows. A well-kept vineyard and orchard surrounded the big, double log cabin. The barn, smokehouse and tobacco shed were freshly whitewashed. The Trent establishment, simple and sturdy, bespoke long hours of hard labor and a rigidity of conscience that never left a weed unhoed.

On the Kumlien side of the fence, wild raspberries and blackberries grew in the summer months, making a cheerful tangle. Birds of many varieties built their hidden nests. The fence row blended into the virgin forest, green in spring, gold, crimson and leather-brown in autumn. Sixty of Kumlien's eighty acres were untouched wilderness.

Just now, with a quilt of new snow trying to bridge the differences between these two farms, there was still a grim severity on the Trent side, and a promise of new adventure in the oak openings and protective thickets across the fence. In the twenty acres which Kumlien cultivated, the dry corn of the previous autumn still stood uneven in the rows, uncut, unshocked and unhusked except for the immediate need of Professor Kumlien's cow, his two pigs and his team of aging oxen. Rabbits and squirrels, prairie chickens and partridges knew where to find an easy meal. Their tracks were everywhere.

Music seldom came from the Trent cabin. Robbie's mother had sung and played the organ in her girlhood. But she seldom sang so much as a hymn these days. By contrast, music was woven all through the woods and weeds of the Kumlien acreage. Not only the songs of the birds—now mostly silenced by winter—but the pure notes of Thure Kumlien's flute, and the rich chords of his youngest son's guitar.

When Robbie and his dog reached the liberating stile over the rail fence between the farms, Old Tessie sniffed the air critically and barked a clear warning.

"What's bothering you, Tessie?" the boy asked.

The dog whined.

"A wolf?"

Tessie set off a volley of barks. Then she tipped her muzzle toward the sky and howled mournfully. The howl was immediately answered from very near at hand by such a long-drawn wail as never emerges from the throat of any dog. It had the sadness of centuries of hunger and persecution, the loneliness of winter winds howling around a cabin far from civilization. Robbie had heard this sound many times in his twelve years. There was no mistaking it. This was the howl of the wolf he had heard before dawn.

Tessie put her tail between her legs and began to shiver. She was such a picture of misery that Robbie felt deep compassion for the faithful old dog. She had been brave in her youth and had given many years of good service. But she was old and tired now, deserving her well-earned rest beside the fire.

"All right," the boy said, "you can go home!" He waved his hand in the direction of the Trent cabin. Tessie yipped her joy. She ran around Robbie in circles. She bowed, laughing gratefully with her eyes and with her lolling tongue. She seemed almost young again.

"Go on, Tessie. I'm not afeared."

And off she ran, limping only slightly from the old wolf wound on her hip. Robbie needed a few moments to reflect before plunging down the path through Kumlien's woods.

He climbed the stile and sat on the top step from which he had a sweeping view of the domain he called his own, Lake Koshkonong stretching eleven miles from inlet to outlet, the ice still firm and covered with new snow to the far shore. Low hills wooded with oaks and hickories and maples came down to bayous and marshes where in season wild rice and wild celery furnished a rich harvest for the water birds. From the sandy beaches and lowland pastures, the fields rose gently to acreage for corn, wheat and tobacco.

But Robbie could not concentrate on the scene before him. The wolf still wailed through his mind. With all his heart he wished that he owned a young, adventuresome dog—one who could help Tessie with the chores, and could accompany Robbie himself on his explorations of the Eden spread out before him.

At last his breath came regularly again and his heart ceased its thumping. "I'm not afeared of any old wolf," he said, as he jumped from the stile and started down the path toward the Busseyville post office.

The wolf's tracks crossed and recrossed the trail. "A big one," Robbie thought seeing the five-inch imprints. "Afeared" or not, he hastened his pace toward the village ahead.

Even without such a welcome event as a wolf in the woods, Robbie's Saturday excursion to Busseyville was the high point in his week.

He was fascinated by the busy settlement. Here at the center of a dozen scattered houses stood the two ivy-covered stone mills, one on each bank of Koshkonong Creek. Both used the waters of the millpond to turn moss-covered water wheels.

On the near bank stood the gristmill with its bins and hoppers for grain, its heavy millstones, between which were ground corn meal for johnnycake, wheat for home-made bread, and buckwheat flour for flapjacks eaten with butter and maple syrup.

On the far bank stood the sawmill which cut the logs of the region into boards for the new houses and barns. It was always a joy to jump into the pile of fragrant sawdust or to watch the sawyer expertly shunting his logs through and past the huge circular saw.

The grumbling of the millstones on one side of the creek and the whining and screeching of the saw on the other blended with the splash of water in the buckets of the slow-turning water wheels to make a harmony sweeter to Robbie than the music of harps.

Below the dam was a dark, deep fishing hole where walleyed pike, black bass and mighty pickerel hit almost any bait or lure.

More romantic than either of the mills were the general store and post office. Here farmers and loafers gathered to do their whittling and storytelling. The store itself was loaded with "plunder" that would pleasure any boy: stag-handled jackknives with as many as six blades, bamboo fishing poles, sturdy green fish lines, big red and green bobbers, and hooks large enough to hold the heaviest fish in Lake Koshkonong. There was every sort of candy imaginable in the rows of big glass jars: striped peppermints, horehound and black licorice whips. You could spend every penny you had if you weren't careful.

The fragrances were what his father would have called "a joy unto the Lord" and also to Robbie. The open barrel of pickles, which were constantly being sampled, smelled sharply of dill and brine. Salt codfish, smoked hams, coffee beans, tea leaves, spices and herbs of every kind known to the spice trade and to the herb garden combined exotically to tantalize the nostrils.

There was food for the mind as well as for the stomach. You could usually buy copies of *Harper's Illustrated Weekly, The Toledo Blade,* and *The New York Tribune.* Ephraim Bussey averred that anyone who read the periodicals he sold in his emporium could be as up-to-date as any New Yorker and as well-informed politically as the late Horace Greeley.

But the pigeonholes for the mail demonstrated most perfectly the cosmopolitan aspect of this rural village. Although some of the citizens could scarcely read and write, they anxiously awaited letters sent to them by loved ones in the countries from which they had come. Robbie always looked for missives from Totley, a village in Derbyshire, England, from which his father had emigrated. German and Scandinavian postmarks were common.

Professor Kumlien, the all but penniless naturalist, received the most intriguing mail. He often showed it to his young friend and disciple Robbie, who, after all, was professionally concerned. It was Robbie who found and purloined many of the birds' eggs the Professor sold to egg collectors and to the great museums of the world. Boy and man were grossly underpaid for this difficult and exacting work.

Kumlien was standing at the mail counter as Robbie entered.

"Anything for me from Leyden, Holland?"

"Not a thing, Professor."

"A ship that never comes to port!" Thure Kumlien murmured. The trim shoulders of the blond and blue-eyed man sagged a little. The homespun coat that his wife Margretta had carded, spun, dyed, woven and fashioned from their own wool looked older and more shabby.

"Why a letter from Leyden?" Robbie asked quietly. The serious, dark-eyed boy realized that the naturalist was disappointed.

"Well, Robbie, you remember that shipment of one hundred and thirty-eight mounted birds I sent to the Royal Museum in Leyden last year?"

"With the birds' nests and the blown eggs?"

"It arrived in Leyden safely enough, but they've never sent a dollar nor a guilder."

"Do you think they are trying to cheat you?"

"No," Kumlien said, "but they might postpone payment until Margretta and I are both dead!"

Although the potbellied stove in the Busseyville store was glowing, Robbie was suddenly chilled. Thure Kumlien dead? But who would teach him, if his friend were gone? Who would take him to the dank-smelling tamarack swamp where the wild orchids grew—the pink and white Indian moccasin, the little yellow lady's-slipper and Kumlien's favorite of all flowers, the large, delicately scented and rare Arethusa?

On looking up, Robbie was surprised to find Professor Kumlien no longer somber.

"Look what came from Boston, Robbie!" Into the

boy's cupped hands, Kumlien poured a cascade of little jewels—muted shades of red, yellow, off-white, amber and deep brown, circles within circles, within ovals.

"The eyes," Robbie gloated, "the glass eyes!"

"Small and exquisite enough for the ruby-throated hummingbird, large and fierce enough for the bald eagle."

"There's a pair for your red-eyed vireo," Robbie said, "and two more for the American goldeneye."

Not many of the settlers in that village store were interested in glass eyes for mounted birds, but they listened with reluctant fascination when Thure Kumlien talked. They could not understand a syllable of the Latin names he gave to plants and birds, but they were vaguely aware that the gentle Swede understood mysteries they would never fathom. They were slightly contemptuous of this unsuccessful farmer—a plowman who would leave his plow in the furrow with his oxen chewing their cuds, while he followed a bird or butterfly into the next township. But they came to beg his freely given services when they wanted a letter written in almost any language of the old country.

"Knows too much for his own good!" was the usual verdict of these wheat and tobacco farmers. But they were glad enough to get his help in surveying their land.

At fifty-three there was something almost boyish about this young-old man. His hands were as work-hardened as their own, and there were lines of weariness in his handsome face. But there was also an air of great alertness and intelligent curiosity.

Robbie and Thure pulled on flannel-lined, cowskin mittens, preparing to launch forth into the raw February day.

"Don't forget your salt and yard goods," the storekeeper called.

"Of course," Thure agreed, "how forgetful!"

"That will be eighty-seven cents."

"But I thought the butter and eggs I brought . . ."

"Don't come to enough."

Kumlien searched his pockets. He pulled them inside out

to show that he had no money. But the village merchant did not laugh. "I want to talk to you, Professor."

Thure knew what Ephraim Bussey wanted to discuss. So did most of the loafers around the stove. The store was suddenly so quiet you could hear the Seth Thomas clock ticking faithfully in the corner.

"About my credit, I suppose!"

"Yes, sir, about your credit."

Among the idlers, the man in the captain's chair strained his ears the most avidly. He wore a coat and hat which had cost several bobcats their lives, a coat that would turn back any blizzard. Opened now to admit the heat of the stove, it revealed a jacket of wide checks and a waistcoat of crimson satin, slightly stained, crossed by a heavy watch chain of yellow gold. He picked his teeth contemplatively with a gold-stemmed goose quill.

Snatches of Kumlien's explanations could be heard by the men. "Money due from Leyden . . . Two hundred dollars a term from Albion Academy . . . lumber needed for the new house."

"Reckon I could help you out, Professor" said the man with the bobcat coat and yellow eyes. "Course I ain't graduated from no university. Don't know the fancy Latin names of any of them varmints you stuff."

"Are you suggesting a loan?" Thure Kumlien asked.

"Cost you three percent a month," Zeke Mooney said.

"Three percent a month is . . . thirty-six percent a year." Robbie Trent was surprised to hear his own angry voice breaking in upon this adult conversation. "And thirty-six percent is usury."

"Smart boy," said Zeke.

"Thank you, Robbie," said Thure Kumlien. "Your arithmetic is improving."

"Tell him you don't want money from any thieving old fur trader," Robbie said in an audible stage whisper.

"Wait a minute, Robbie," said the slightly embarrassed naturalist. "Zeke was offering me a business proposition. Everybody here knows I am poor. And everyone knows that Mr. Mooney has money to lend. . . ."

"He cheated me on my furs," Robbie whispered fiercely to his friend. "And he cheats every trapper on the lake. I hate him. I hate his son, Bubs. I hate their mean white dog." Kumlien's hand, tousling Robbie's hair, eased the tension.

"Thank you very much," Kumlien said. "But I'm sure Ephraim will carry me for the usual twelve percent a year."

"Well," Bussey paused, "since you've got regular employment at the academy . . ."

The idlers were not ill-pleased by this exchange. Zeke Mooney's conniving was known to them all. The fur trader flushed slightly, fastened his coat, pulled on his gloves and moved silently from the room.

Fifteen minutes later, their business finished with the storekeeper, Thure and Robbie again prepared to leave.

"Remember me to Margretta," Bussey's plump wife called cheerily. "How is she doing these days?"

"Not very well, I'm afraid."

"Is there anything I can do to help her?"

"There's nothing much any of us can do," the Professor said thoughtfully, "except maybe build the house she has always dreamed about."

"Everybody would come to a spring house-raising," Mary Bussey said. "And soon it *will* be spring with the wild geese coming north and the violets blooming."

"Yes, it will soon be spring." A faraway look came into Thure Kumlien's eyes as he and Robbie stepped out into the chill.

As they walked westward up the trail, leaving the village of Busseyville behind them, Kumlien took a handful of sunflower seeds from his pocket. He had spotted several black-capped chickadees companionably flitting along beside them in the bushes. He held out his seeds, and paused for a moment until the birds, who knew him well, hovered near. Finally one, bolder than the rest, had the courage to light for a moment on Kumlien's finger. It seized a seed and whirred off in triumph.

"Most birds and beasts are friendly, if you give them a chance."

"Chickadees, yes. But how about timber wolves? Won't they attack a man?"

"I really don't think so," Kumlien said thoughtfully.

"But all the story books say . . ."

"Yes, Robbie, but those old fables are about European wolves."

"Are American wolves different?"

"It would seem so. I've never been bitten, nor has any other settler I've heard of."

"That's good," the boy said, "because there's a big wolf in the woods."

They had not progressed a dozen rods when, as though to confirm the statement, there came a series of yips and a long wavering howl.

"That's a timber wolf all right," Kumlien said. "Listen and don't move. . . . I think it's a mating female. Maybe we can see her."

As a flutist, he knew that the cry had begun on middle C, had glided up the chromatic scale about eight half notes and had broken to the C above, there to commence the diminishing downward wail.

There was no answering howl, as might have come had there been a pair or a pack, but there *was* the eager baying of Kumlien's big dog Ring, himself part wolf.

They knew their local dogs so well that Robbie could say with conviction, "That isn't Ring's *hunting* cry."

"No, it isn't."

"What is Ring saying to that wolf?"

Kumlien chuckled. "Maybe he's saying, 'I love you.' *Canis familiaris* pursuing *Canis lupus*."*

The wolf howl echoed again, with Ring's ardent baying intermingled.

"I'm not afeared of any wolf," Robbie said again, as though it were an incantation to ward off wolf bite.

---

* Thure Kumlien knew all the creatures of southern Wisconsin by their scientific Latin names, but to avoid pedantry I have omitted much of the Latin.

"The word is 'afraid' Robbie. You know that."

"Well I'm not afraid then."

"Good," Kumlien said softly, "because they're coming down that ridge not fifty feet away."

At this moment they appeared, moving swiftly. The pale gray wolf in full winter pellage seemed to float by, with Ring, black as sable, not twenty feet behind. For one memorable instant they were fixed in time and space before they disappeared into the foggy woods beyond.

Robbie ran ahead eagerly, with Kumlien following.

"Notice anything unusual about her tracks?" the naturalist asked.

"She's a big wolf."

"Yes, she is. But look at this print of her right front foot."

"Why, she's only got three toes on that paw," Robbie said.

"You're learning, Robbie."

"We'll call her 'Old Three Toes,' " Robbie said. "Poor thing, she must have been in a trap."

"You're learning with your heart as well as your head."

"Will they mate? Will they have whelps?"

"Very likely."

"How long before the pups come?"

"About sixty-three days."

"Golly, Professor Kumlien, you know *everything*."

"I know very little," the man said. "It has taken me a lifetime to learn how little even the greatest experts know about nature."

"Suppose I can find the den, and suppose I can capture a whelp, do you suppose my father would let me keep him?"

"That's a lot of 'supposes,' " the Professor said.

"Is it hard to find a wolf den?"

"Very hard, Robbie. And even harder to get a pup out of the den."

"I'll do it," Robbie said, "if it is the last thing I do in my whole life."

"Good luck, son. You've got your spring work cut out for you."

2: Waiting for Old Three Toes

Like most farm boys of the era, Robbie Trent was expected to help his father with both the morning and the evening chores, and on Saturdays to accomplish two-thirds the work of a full-grown man. Both his father and his mother worked very hard. Robbie felt no resentment about carrying his just share of the load. Meanwhile his mind was free to roam the woods and to imagine the joy of finding and capturing a wolfling.

Robbie did not tell his parents about his project. From long experience he knew exactly what they would say:

"A pet wolf on a farm where sheep are raised?"

"Are you crazy, lad?"

His mother would be a little more gentle, a trifle more consoling. But Robbie must plan very shrewdly if he wished a wolf whelp for a companion.

During the sixty-three days that Robbie marked on his calendar in the loft, the great globe curved one-sixth of its way around the distant sun. The boy knew from what he had been told by Professor Kumlien that the miracle of spring was due to the tilt of the earth, and the greater abundance of sunlight now lavished upon the Northern Hemisphere. This light and warmth first melted the snows of winter. It sent a stir of life into the seeds and roots of grass and flowers, pulled the sweet sap of the sugar maples to the very tips of the budding branches. It stimulated the water birds and songsters into their seasonal migration northward, and told the wolves and many other animals that it was time to mate and to bring forth their young.

One of the first whispers of spring in southern Wisconsin was the February thaw which brought the silent mist creeping up the river to engulf the valley of Lake Koshkonong. The tobacco plants which had been hanging, dry and brittle, in the tobacco sheds, now softened until the leaves were like thin brown leather.

"Case weather!" Ezra Trent shouted, as he lit the lantern early on a foggy morning.

"Coming, Paw," Robbie answered from the loft.

"Must it always be in the middle of the night?" Ellen murmured sleepily. But she too was soon out of bed and dressed.

Father, mother and dutiful son now moved by lantern light through the hollow in the mist. It was as though they were encased in an endless shadow world where the only reality was a small room, dimly lit by the swinging lantern. It brought them together in one of the tasks that Robbie greatly loved.

Robbie was by far the most agile, and proud of his prowess. He scrambled to the highest beams in the tobacco shed to hand to his father, on a lower level, the laden laths, each with six plants of tobacco, skewered through at the heavy end of the stem. On the earthen floor of the shed, his mother reached upward to take the laths from her husband. These laths of moist tobacco plants were piled, log-cabin fashion, and covered with burlap sacks to retain their moisture and pliability.

In the days to come, Ezra, Ellen and Robbie would take the tobacco, lath by lath, to the "stripping shed," where the leaves were stripped from the stalks and pressed in bundles for transportation to the tobacco buyers in nearby Edgerton. In all of this the Trent family moved in harmony and unity as in some slow ballet.

The next development of spring was also a family project, and once more the night was dark and misty.

From the sheepfold came an unmistakable bleating.

"Lambing time!" Ezra called as he lit the lantern.

"I'll be down in a minute, Paw."

"Again, in the middle of the night!" Ellen sighed. But in no time at all she was heating kettles of water on the kitchen stove, warming clean sacks in the oven and wrapping a shawl around her head.

Working together almost wordlessly, they helped the laboring ewes to bring forth their young, dried the shivering lambs with the warmed feed sacks and helped them to find the full teats of their mothers. No lambs were orphaned this year. No mother refused her offspring or butted an unwanted twin into the corner of the fold. Exhausted but unified by the hard night's work, they made their tired way to the cabin.

In bed once more, but too excited to sleep, Robbie heard a disturbing, whispered conversation.

He knew he should not be listening. But with only the pine flooring between the loft and the room below, many "loft children" of the frontier heard things not meant for their young ears.

"Lass, will you never change your mind?"

"Whatever are you thinking?" Ellen asked, evasively.

"You know what I am thinking."

"A woman does not bear children as ewes bear lambs."

"But Robbie needs brothers and sisters," her husband whispered.

"Three of our four died in the cradle," Ellen reminded him.

"The Lord gave, and the Lord hath taken away."

"That is so easy for a man to say, so hard for a woman to accept."

"You spoil the one that lived," Ezra whispered accusingly.

"I do not spoil Robbie. He needs some time with his books and in God's green world."

" 'For, lo! the winter is past . . . , and the voice of the turtle is heard in our land.' "

"Yes, it *is* spring. But I am mortally tired," Ellen said. "Good night, Ezra."

"Good night, Ellen." His voice was sad and resigned.

Robbie thought he knew now why his father had

turned, more and more, to reading his Bible. And he realized with a wisdom far beyond his age that it is not easy to be a father or a mother.

Ezra Trent had come from Derbyshire, England.

The Kumliens had eloped from Uppsala, Sweden.

The strong young Englishman, like the two romantic Swedes, had little money. They could none of them afford comfortable cabins on the swift packet ships, but came instead on old and leaking vessels which were lucky to survive the ocean crossing.

The port of New York was colorful, dangerous and dirty in the 1840's. Foreign seamen, some with brass rings in their ears, roamed the town. Pigs scavenged in the streets, nosing and scattering the piles of garbage. There were a few hundred gracious houses, but thousands of slums and tenements. Horse-drawn traffic clattered and roared.

Most immigrants were only too happy to leave the city behind and to glide up the majestic Hudson on gaudily painted side-wheelers. Near Albany they transferred themselves and their luggage to mule-drawn canal boats which moved at a leisurely pace across New York State to Buffalo, where the newcomers again changed to Great Lakes vessels.

In the year 1843, Trent and the Kumliens (although on different ships) arrived at the small lake port of Milwaukee. From there they walked westward some seventy miles to Lake Koshkonong. The virgin forests of huge deciduous trees were interspersed with oak openings and small prairies where the deer grazed almost undisturbed except by a few prowling wolves or an occasional panther or black bear.

To Thure and Margretta Kumlien, the wild flowers were incredibly beautiful. They thrilled to every blossom, beast and bird. The youthful Kumlien was already a well-trained botanist and ornithologist. But many of the American flowers and birds were unknown to him. With great excitement and diligence, however, he soon learned their English and Latin names.

Ezra Trent prudently chose the eastern margin of Albion Prairie for his farm. Here few trees needed to be cut, and the soil was deep and fertile. He staked out 160 acres for which he paid the Federal Government $1.25 an acre.

Thure Kumlien, more interested in the natural sciences than in farming, preferred the eighty heavily wooded acres immediately to the east of the Trent property. Here were birds of many varieties, woodland plants and flowers to be botanized, and a far view of Lake Koshkonong across the teeming and marshy meadow. Ezra Trent preferred to conquer the wilderness, Thure Kumlien to embrace and cherish it.

Their contrasting choices of land were typical of their characters, and in a very real sense molded their respective fortunes.

Breaking new land with a sixteen-ox breaking plow was difficult enough even for a young giant like Ezra Trent plowing rolling prairie land. But cutting enormous oaks and hickories, grubbing stumps and turning forest soil was a heartbreaking, backbreaking torment for the willowy and gentle naturalist. He soon was trying to make a meager living by mounting birds and collecting birds' eggs and nests for museums in Europe and America.

Thure Kumlien had thrown away his patrimony, and his chances of preferment at the Royal Court of Sweden, to marry the beautiful but "socially inferior" Margretta Wallberg. The wedding had been opposed by his father, by the church and by the King. Almost penniless, they had cast their luck on a far shore in the forests of southern Wisconsin. There they could be happy or miserable together as fate might decree. They felt as free as the birds while they built their log cabin.

Ezra Trent, on the other hand, worked hard, feared the Lord and waited until he was thirty years old to marry Ellen Douglas, her late father's only heir, a good-looking but sometimes willful girl of sixteen.

All this, of course, was a number of years before Robbie Trent arrived on a night of storm. From a very early age he had envied the first settlers who told of panthers, bears, wolves and deer by the hundreds. It was this long-ing for a "wilder wildness" that urged Robbie to wish to capture a wolfling for a pet. He would rather be an ad-venturer and explorer than a plowboy.

But here he was on a beautiful spring morning, plow-ing his father's land with the two faithful old oxen, Buck and Bright. Robbie preferred the oxen for the same rea-son Thure Kumlien did. They did not walk as fast as the plow horses, and far less rapidly than Spinney, the little Morgan, teamed up with Stonewall, the quick-stepping mule. They plugged along at their own gentle pace, giving Robbie time to search for the nests of quail and prairie chickens, to whistle his answers to bobwhites and to look straight up toward heaven to see whether the long-legged bird sailing over was a sandhill crane or a whooping crane.

A square forty-acre field measures a quarter of a mile on a side. Once around it on the first furrow is a full mile. And to a twelve-year-old boy whose head comes not far above the plow handles, this can be a long walk. His father, who could plow twenty lineal miles a day be-hind his fast-stepping team of dapple grays, Grant and Sherman, expected Robbie to walk at least twelve miles behind the oxen. He had sometimes whipped him for let-ting the oxen stand idle while the young naturalist went hunting birds' nests in Kumlien's woods.

But here came temptation again in the form of Thure Kumlien.

"I've found something to show you, Robbie!"

"Can't, I'll get licked."

"But if it helps you find your wolf?"

"Golly, that's worth a licking."

"It'll take only fifteen or twenty minutes."

"Coming," said Robbie. He left the oxen standing near enough to the little pool so that they could graze on marsh grass and pull over to get a drink of pond water if they became thirsty. It was the one acre of wilderness left on the Trent farm, a bit of bog which was too wet to plow. Whistling happily, Robbie was soon over the fence and off on an adventure with his friend.

Moving along an old Indian trail bordering a little ravine where a trickle of water spilled over mossy stones, they came at last to a huge fallen bur oak, whose heart had rotted out years ago.

"You mean you've found a family of raccoons?" Robbie asked.

"A raccoon family may have visited this hollow log," Kumlien said, "but this fur is what I wanted you to see."

"That's not raccoon fur," Robbie said, "the guard hairs are too long."

"Correct," Kumlien agreed.

"I'll bet it's a wolf," Robbie shouted with joy.

"It might very well be," the Professor said. "It's the right time of year for a wolf to be rubbing off winter pellage."

"Probably Old Three Toes," Robbie said hopefully. "You think she'll have her pups right in this log?"

"Not necessarily," the Professor said. "Wolves usually prepare several dens so that they can move their young if danger threatens."

"How will I *ever* find the *right* den?"

"That's up to you, Robbie. I told you that finding a wolf den is a hard job. But you might try that island in the middle of the tamarack swamp. Right beside the biggest pine at the top of the hill there used to be a den."

"Will you come with me?"

"You aren't afraid of the swamp, are you?" Kumlien asked.

"Well I don't like the place where you wade in. If you get off the sunken lumbering road, you're in quicksand."

"You know your way as well as I do."

"For a wolf whelp I'd go anywhere!"

Kumlien looked at his watch. "Robbie, come home with me for noon dinner. It's Gretta's birthday. Wouldn't you like to pick her a bouquet of these long-stemmed violets? I'll help you."

"I'm afraid I can't stay for dinner. But I would like to bring her a bouquet."

Man and boy had quite forgotten their respective oxen standing in the field. And Robbie had forgotten the whipping he might get. Anyhow, it didn't matter. Maybe it *was* wicked to play hooky. But he probably wouldn't go to heaven in any case. His father had prophesied as much.

"Heaven is right here and now! Isn't that the truth, Mr. Kumlien?"

Kumlien showed no surprise at all at this *non sequitur*. "For so young a naturalist you are very wise, Robbie. That's the only place heaven will *ever* be, right here and now."

When the Professor, followed by Robbie, entered the Kumlien cabin, Margretta came to greet them.

"Look what Robbie has for you."

"You remembered my birthday!"

"I'm afraid I didn't," Robbie said. "Your husband helped me pick these violets."

"You're a good boy, Robbie," Margretta said.

"And painfully honest," Kumlien added.

"I am overwhelmed," Margretta said. "We never make such a fuss over birthdays. First the new rocking chair you made for me, Thure! And now look what the three older children bought me! The greeting reads: 'So Mother will no longer need to fashion by hand all of our clothing. With the love of Ludwig, Theodore and Swea Maria.' "

They all turned toward the corner of the room which had long housed the spinning wheel. There stood a brand-new sewing machine.

"A Wheeler and Wilcox!" Robbie read the gold label with wonder and awe.

"I never thought we would live to be so rich," Thure Kumlien said humbly.

"Now I can make all our clothes with sinful ease," Margretta said, wiping her eyes. "I want to make you a jacket, Thure, a blue student coat with brass buttons. Like the one you wore when you were the brightest student at Uppsala."

"But that is not all," said a voice from the room above. Large feet appeared, followed by long legs, as Frithiof, their youngest son, came down the stairs two at a time.

"It's not a very good portrait of you, Mother, but I have done the best I can."

"It's truly lovely," Margretta said. "You are becoming a fine painter. But you have made me look so young." She hid her tired face in her hands.

"You were very beautiful," her husband said, "and you still are."

"Oh, thank you, thank you," Margretta Christine Kumlien cried. "But why are you all so generous? Is it because . . . because you think it is my last birthday?"

"Nonsense," Thure Kumlien said. "You will have many more birthdays."

"That I doubt," said his wife, turning back to her cooking.

"Surely you will stay for dinner!" Frithiof said to Robbie. "Everyone will be here: Ludwig, Theodore, Swea Maria and Aunt Sophia."

"I must get back to my plowing," Robbie said, "or I'll get a whipping." His mouth watered as he caught the odor of wild duck with sage and mushroom dressing. Mounds of delicious fiddlehead ferns spiced with Margretta's herbs, crab-apple pickles, and a dozen other delicacies proved once again that Mrs. Kumlien was one of the best cooks of the region. Robbie wished that he might stay for dinner.

Thure with his flute and Frithiof with his guitar began to play a Swedish folk song as Robbie reluctantly said his good-byes.

"Happy birthday, Mrs. Kumlien."

"And a fine day to you, Robbie."

No matter what punishment came of this day, Robbie felt that he had glimpsed a small corner of paradise.

Robbie had squandered half the morning before returning to his oxen. They were standing where he had left them, grazing beside the marshy pool.

This "pothole" supported a multitude of life. Bullfrogs croaked. A tiny short-tailed marsh wren popped out of her nest like a cork from a bottle. A male red-winged blackbird, swaying on a cattail, viewed with ecstasy his little principality of seven nests and seven modest brown wives all dutifully sitting on their eggs. He arched his black wings, showing the crimson epaulets on his shoulders, and warbled his joy with a long-drawn "Konkereeeeeeeeee."

Back in the furrow once more, Robbie and the oxen began slowly circling the field. The plow curled a neat ribbon of black earth which flowed from the moldboard in a process so smooth and somnolent that it almost put Robbie to sleep.

The distressing cry of what seemed to be a wounded killdeer brought the boy wide awake. As Robbie well knew, it did *not* have a broken wing. This eleven-inch plover with the two black bands across its breast was putting on a dramatic scene to save its eggs which were laid with no protection among small glacial pebbles. Its beak was open as though it were uttering its last gasp, and its extended wings trailed pitifully in the dust.

"You're just play acting," Robbie said to the bird. He stopped the oxen and began to examine every inch of wheat stubble, walking carefully so as not to crush the eggs accidentally. Experienced as he was, it took Robbie a quarter of an hour to find the four brown-splotched eggs, nestled together in a little depression in the soil. Knowing that the killdeer would replace the egg he was stealing, Robbie took just one of the delightful ovals of potential cry-and-flight. Professor Kumlien would give him five cents or perhaps a dime for this treasure. He plowed carefully around the nest, leaving a small island of stubble in his widening river of black soil.

What with searching for the killdeer egg, stopping to examine a mouse's nest lined with thistledown, poking a stick into a woodchuck hole and keeping his eyes peeled for Indian arrowheads, Robbie made only two more rounds that morning. Added to the one he had completed before being lured into the woods, this was only three rounds—three slow miles behind the plow on that fresh and sunny April day. He whistled cheerfully as he took the oxen to the barn for their "nooning." His plowing had fallen short of his father's schedule, but there had been many compensations. He should have known that ecstasy cannot last forever.

He drove the oxen into the barn, relieved them of their heavy yoke, threw down hay for them and for the horses, the cow and the mule. He was preparing to go in to noon dinner, and was thinking how much he liked his mother's fried chicken, when his father's silhouette enshadowed the doorway.

"Robbie, take off your shirt."

"But, Father!"

"How many rounds?"

"Only three."

"When you could have done six."

Robbie slowly removed his hickory shirt. Despite himself, he trembled. But he was determined not to cry. He would not give his father the satisfaction of hearing him moan. He would never again cry when he was thrashed, even if the blood came. He noticed with relief that his father was taking the buggy whip and not the heavy strap. *That* he could endure.

"Wait, please wait!" Robbie took the precious killdeer egg from his shirt pocket and placed it on the sill of the barn window.

"Ready," he said. The faint strains of flute and guitar music came drifting in from the adjoining farm.

Robbie waited. No blow fell.

He looked up questioningly. He was surprised to see tears in his father's eyes.

Ellen Douglas Trent was at this time a rather handsome, sandy-haired woman in her mid-thirties. This branch of the Douglas clan had for several generations been well-paid "gillies" to Englishmen of wealth. They trained dogs and horses for their employers, managed their hunting boxes in Scotland, tied their salmon flies and in general were the pampered and independent companions of sporting gentlemen in their hours of outdoor leisure.

These superior servants were Scotsmen (or Scotchmen as they preferred to be called); they saved their money, held their heads high and feared no man. When Robert Douglas and his wife Mary decided to move to America, they had many gold crowns to sew into their belts. They were the parents of only one child, Ellen, and they sailed from Liverpool on a beautiful packet that skimmed the waves of the North Atlantic like a gull. They were not taken in by the money-changers in New York who offered them "good American paper for their worthless foreign gold." Nor were they robbed on the Hudson River, or the Erie Canal, or the Great Lakes.

Unlike the Kumliens and the Trents, who had walked the seventy miles from Milwaukee, they had hired a driver with a light spring wagon to convey them, promising to pay all damages for springs and wheels that might be injured along the half-broken trail.

The 320-acre farm that they bought from the government was not very fertile. Almost half of it was woods and water so that Robert could continue hunting and fishing while somebody else did his farming. His uneven land proved better for grazing sheep than for corn and wheat. Like most of his kind, he deplored level land and preferred hills and dales, being lonesome for his native heather.

Mary, who had taken ill on the crossing, soon died.

Without the companionship and diplomatic restraint of his beloved Mary, Robert drank heavily and went through most of his gold. His thirteen-year-old daughter Ellen took over the management of the household. She learned how to churn butter, make soap from wood ashes and tallow, card, spin, dye and weave the wool from their sheep. Robert never lost his love for dogs or his ability to train them. He taught his daughter his lore of training sheep dogs. Old Tessie, whom Ellen later schooled, could be directed with a few whistles and hand signals to make a flock of sheep go over bridges, through gates into and out of the dipping trough, or anywhere else her owner wanted. The old dog could practically take care of a flock without human help.

Robert outlived his wife by three years, then died in a hunting accident. Ellen, his only child and heir, was at that time sixteen years of age. She knew whom she wanted and she got him. Ezra Trent was not very handsome. But he was strong, sober, hard-working and reliable, and he owned a very fertile 160 acres. They were married in the little Methodist church on Albion Prairie and moved into the large double log cabin, with gallery between, that Ezra had built of hewn white oak logs. Ellen sold her father's infertile farm and put the additional gold coins under a secret stone of her new hearth. Ezra did not question her right to do so.

Having been an only child herself, Ellen wanted her children to be multiple. But after two boys and a beautiful little girl had been born and had died in infancy, she concluded that God was more stubborn than she was.

She decided to try once more. So Robbie came into the world and was more treasured because of the loss of the others.

Ellen believed that gold, being a precious commodity, must be used to buy equally precious articles, such as a kerosene lamp, where before there had been only candles, and a cooking stove to eliminate the endless stooping over the fireplace.

If she could not give her husband many sons, she could, for about seventy-five cents a day, hire an endless procession of strong but unemployed men who were now drifting westward—German and Scandinavian immigrants on the way to settle Minnesota and the Dakotas, ex-soldiers, restless and aimless and wandering.

There were bunks in the "out-cabin" as they called the southern wing of the house. And Ellen was able and willing to feed the young men and wash their clothes if they would accept her terms of payment. They stayed a day, a week or maybe a month, and were remembered only as Heinrich or Eric or John or the one with the missing ear. Robbie often wished they would stay longer and tell more of their stories. He also appreciated the fact that they furnished part of the field labor, thus making it possible for him to have a rare half-holiday in the woods.

It was Robbie, not Ellen, who discovered the most important thing that money can buy, which is time for yourself. Time to study the birds and animals and flowers. Time to walk in the deep timber, or row on the lake.

Money which boys earned in those days was frequently appropriated by their fathers. To risk a repetition, it cannot be too strongly emphasized that a boy's time belonged to his father until the boy was twenty-one years of age. Sometimes young men "bought their time" so that they could go to college or merely escape and start living their own lives before their majority. Robbie, being an only child, was indulged in being allowed to keep the money he made trapping muskrats, or selling birds' nests and eggs to Kumlien.

One evening he asked his father how much the work of a boy of twelve was worth.

"Twenty-five or maybe fifty cents a day, if he's a willing worker. Why do you ask? Do you expect me to pay you?"

"No, I want to pay *you*," Robbie said, watching his father's face a trifle fearfully. "I want to buy my time."

His father's face darkened with anger. Ellen, too, was caught by surprise.

"Not when you really need me," Robbie hurried on, "not in haying time or tobacco harvest time or on butchering days or when the lambs are borning."

His mother asked a practical question. "How much money do you have, Robbie?"

"Four dollars," the boy said proudly, "and I'm worth fifty cents a day—because I really *am* a good worker— that would buy me eight whole days." The prospect absolutely dazzled him, and his face by lamplight was radiant.

"Well, Ezra?" his mother's voice was tender.

"You tricked me into it," his father said, his stern mouth showing a trace of a smile. "Robbie, you take after your mother more than a little bit."

On the very next Saturday, Robbie took a shining half dollar from the hoard which he had hidden in a sock beneath his cornhusk mattress. At breakfast he placed it beside his father's plate.

"What are you planning, Robbie?"

"I want to buy my day."

"Whatever for?"

"For a walk in the woods," Robbie said.

Ezra looked searchingly at his wife. Her eyes were gently pleading. But the scowl on Ezra's face foreboded no weakening.

"Now look here, son," his father said. "A deal is a deal, but you yourself said, 'Not in haying time or tobacco harvest time or on butchering days or when the lambs are borning.'"

"It's none of those days," Robbie said.

"But we're behind in our spring work," his father said.

"Paw, I just got to have this day."

"Give me one good reason why."

"I can't tell you," Robbie said desperately, knowing that the little wolves were probably three days old and that he still had not found the den. "Don't you trust me?"

"Of course we trust you," his mother said.

"Now, Ellen, you stay out of this. Robbie, I can't spare you today. Hitch up Spinney and Stonewall and start dragging the back forty. Corn planting time is catching up with us and the land isn't near ready."

So Robbie walked in the deep tilth behind the drag, thinking and dreaming about the wolf whelp he might never get. Someone else might find the den and knock the wolf pups on the head and collect the bounty. He looked up at the sky and said, "What am I going to do, God?"

"Try Sunday!" the Great Voice seemed to say.

"Sunday?" Robbie asked incredulously. "Why that's Your day, God."

"I guess I can give you my day if I want to."

So Robbie went to bed very tired but very happy, and at breakfast the next morning he hesitantly asked his father if he could take a walk in the woods, even if it was Sunday.

"'Remember the sabbath day to keep it holy.'"

"I remember, Father. How could I possibly forget?" Robbie murmured sadly.

"'Six days shalt thou labour and do all thy work.' Now, where do we find that in the Bible, son?"

"The Book of Exodus, Chapter Twenty, verses eight and nine," Robbie replied without enthusiasm. "After Sunday school and church, I just want to walk in the woods."

"And you won't carry a gun or a fish pole?"

"I won't do anything wicked."

"Well," Ezra Trent hesitated, "if you're back in time for the evening chores."

"Golly, thanks! I'll be home in plenty of time for evening chores."

All through Sunday school and throughout the morning sermon, Robbie's mind wandered far from the text, far from the small white church where the preacher seemed to drone on interminably.

When they returned from church, Robbie made a fast change into overalls, swiftly consumed the dinner Ellen had cooked (no rest for the women on Sunday) and in another two minutes had hurdled the Kumlien fence and was loping down the old Indian trail northward toward the tamarack swamp. The many entrancing sounds, which might have slackened his pace on any other day, now slowed him not at all—a ruffed grouse booming on his log, a flame-crested eighteen-inch pileated woodpecker chopping on a dead tree, even the barking of a red fox, sharp, high and inquiring. On this particular Sunday, dedicated to the investigation of the island in the tamarack swamp, no everyday miracle of nature could divert him from his purpose.

For nearly a mile Robbie followed the wooded valley of Koshkonong Creek, startling an occasional blue heron. He did notice in passing that a family of otters was "pleasuring" itself, even though it *was* Sunday. The sleek, handsome creatures were enjoying their favorite pastime of chuting down their smooth mud slides into the water and climbing the bank again for another run.

Crossing the winding creek on a big fallen elm, the boy soon came to the ice-cold, coffee-colored rivulet which emerged from the tamarack swamp. This he traced to its source among the dark green conifers. There he found to his dismay that a colony of beavers had dammed the outlet, raising the level of the water nearly three feet.

Robbie was a brave, bright twelve-year-old. Later he would become a strong swimmer, but as yet he could scarcely keep himself afloat. Boys of that region in the 1870's were "held to the plow" for so many days of the spring, and to the cultivator, hoe and hay fork so many days of the summer, that frequently they had no opportunity to learn to swim.

The old lumbering road (over which Kumlien had previously led him) had a rock-fill base, bordered by quicksand. Formerly this abandoned trail had been no more than a foot under water. Now, due to the work of the beavers, it was nearly four feet beneath the surface. Somewhat dismayed, but still determined to reach the island, Robbie took off his clothes, and holding them above his head, began wading. Knee-deep, hip-deep, waist-deep! The cold water, stained by the tamarack roots, crept up his shivering body. Shoulder-deep, neck-deep! Another eight or ten inches might have proved fatal. But now the road tilted upward toward the island. With a fervent word of thanks to his Creator, Robbie reached solid land in safety, swiftly dressed and began to mount the fascinating little hill.

The glacial moraine which formed this green circle was a veritable botanical garden. Sphagnum moss grew to the water's edge. A little farther up the slope was to be found the only trailing arbutus in this area, its evergreen leaves making a perfect background for the fragrant clusters of pink, five-petaled flowers. Other delights were more varieties of wild orchids than in any other part of southern Wisconsin.

But this was no day to botanize. Robbie gave little more than a passing glance to the flowers which garlanded this island among the tamaracks. Struggling through the thicket, he came at last to the very summit of the hill where stood a great pine, gnarled and splendid. Had its trunk been straight (and thus valuable to the lumbermen) it would have been felled some years before. True to Kumlien's prediction, near the foot of this tree

was the den of a wolf. Robbie's heart thumped with anticipation as he kneeled to peer into the dark tunnel. Sand had been excavated to form a wide mound in front of the entrance. Was this the home of the mother wolf and her newborn whelps? (The water that surrounded the island formed no obstacle to Old Three Toes. As Kumlien had explained, wolves swim very well and frequently catch and eat fish.)

But Robbie had been well-trained to analyze the wilderness evidence. There were tracks in this fresh soil. There were even the thrilling, three-toed tracks for which he was seeking. But all of them were *several weeks old,* the edges blurred by more than one rainstorm. Sadly Robbie concluded that the mother wolf had merely deepened this hole for a safe retreat in case of danger.

He had lost one more precious day, and the possibility of capturing a wolf puppy seemed more remote than ever.

But Robbie would not admit defeat. As Miss Hitchcock so often said: "If at first you don't succeed, try, try again."

3: The Osprey and the Eagle

Hannah Hitchcock was the tough but tender, grim but affectionate teacher of the one-room school near Busseyville. She was slightly more than six feet tall, angular and fearless. She was gentle and protective toward the smaller children, but undaunted by the eighth-grade bullies. Born of New England stock, she was also the living representative of the New England virtues. With the help of McGuffey's *Readers,* Webster's *Speller* and Ray's *Arithmetic,* the children learned their reading, writing and ciphering or felt the stinging rap of Hannah's heavy ruler.

Formidable as she seemed to older mischief-makers, she was a guardian angel to toddlers who turned to her for comfort. She was a close friend of Margarethe Meyer Schurz—Mrs. Carl Schurz—who founded the first kindergarten in America in nearby Watertown. Because Hannah's schoolroom was one of the best behaved in the county, it was also one of the liveliest and most progressive. Miss Hitchcock, born in Concord, Massachusetts, had been a girlhood playmate of Louisa May Alcott. She recalled that her friend "could roll a hoop faster and farther" than any girl in the village, and "jumped fences as well as any boy."

She had met, as a child, Emerson, Hawthorne and Longfellow, and could describe them so vividly that her scholars felt they themselves had known these great men of letters. Once, with Louisa Alcott, she had visited Thoreau, who always welcomed children who came to his little cabin on Walden Pond.

The eighth graders, all four of them, had graduated at a ceremony held on the previous Friday. Somehow the absence of these overgrown near-adults gave the rest of the children a sense of relief and release. And since this was the last day of school before the summer vacation, the occasion was a merry one.

"No lessons on this final day," Miss Hitchcock said.

Cheers!

"But I would like to hear the recitations you have been learning."

Groans!

"Who would like to begin?"

Celeste Henderson, a pretty redhead, who had the best croquet set, the only pony cart, and many fancy dresses, raised her hand and was acknowledged. She curtsied to the class and said:

> "Lives of great men all remind us
> We can make our lives sublime,
> And, departing, leave behind us
> Footprints on the sands of time."

"Thank you, Celeste. Next?"

Bubs Mooney, barefoot, slingshot only slightly concealed in the hip pocket of his overalls, raised his hand.

"I ain't got no recitation," he said.

"You mean you have no recitation."

"You catch on quick, Miss Hitchcock."

The children giggled. Hannah Hitchcock rapped for order.

"The next time you are saucy, Bubs Mooney, I'll rap you with my ruler. Now who wishes to be next?"

Ingeborg Skavilain raised her hand, and Robbie Trent immediately began to forget his passage from Emerson's *Self-Reliance*. There was something about that pig-tailed towhead with her faint sprinkling of honest freckles that addled Robbie's wits and made his heart turn somersaults. Inga was reciting the craziest poem in McGuffey, "The Wreck of the Hesperus," but to Robbie it might have been Shelley, Byron and Keats all rolled into one. She was the most carefree tomboy on the one hand, and the saddest little girl on the other. Robbie didn't know what to make of her.

They all said their good-byes at last, fastened their books and slates in their book straps, promised to be back in the fall and set off on their various paths toward home. For a little way Robbie and Inga could walk together, and she let him carry her books. He knew he did not in any way deserve such happiness.

Where their paths parted, she skipped off, with a saucy flip of her pigtails.

"See you next autumn, Robbie."

But by uncontrived coincidence they were to meet the very next morning.

Upon parting, Robbie thought about Inga for three faithful minutes, then was diverted by an osprey with a majestic wingspread. The big fish hawk looked almost as large as an eagle but was white underneath, whereas eagles are dark in these regions. There were other differences also. The osprey had a slight bend in his wings. Eagles, as Robbie knew, soar on level pinions.

The osprey was peacefully fishing, gliding in circles over Lake Koshkonong. Suddenly he dove from at least one hundred feet, hit the water with a splash, which sent sparkling jets into the sunshine, and emerged from the lake clutching a fish in his strong talons. As usual he carried the fish headfirst, to "split the wind" as he flew toward his nest.

Five hundred feet above him, an eagle saw the whole maneuver. His power dive was much faster than the osprey's. Robbie knew he was watching aerial piracy, but he could not help being thrilled by the ferocious robber who now plummeted out of the blue. The bald eagle who was determined to steal the fish was a mature bird. His head, neck and tail were a dazzling white. His hooked beak and curved talons were an open challenge to the osprey, a bird who by some ancient covenant with the eagle, at such a time drops his hard-earned fish to save his own life. But the big fish hawk was a moment too slow in releasing his prize. The outraged eagle struck him a blow in passing which drove one talon through the osprey's heart. The larger bird then continued his plunge to retrieve the fish before it could hit the ground.

Robbie was beneath the mortally wounded osprey, which fluttered to earth not far from his feet. The boy picked up the warm body and admired the gray, brown and snowy-white feathers.

Saddened for only a moment by this sudden death, Robbie was solaced by the opportunity of bringing such a bird to Kumlien. He hastened eagerly down the path and found the naturalist working at the sturdy table beside his doorstep.

"Hello, Professor Kumlien!"

"Hello, Robbie, what have you there? Why, it's an osprey."

"Isn't it a beauty?"

"A magnificent specimen."

Taking the wing tips between the thumb and forefinger of each hand, Kumlien spread them as widely as he could spread his arms. "Five and a half feet at least. Who killed it, Robbie?"

"That old bald eagle," Robbie said. "The osprey was too slow in dropping the fish."

"I need an osprey," the Professor said. "Agassiz of Boston wants one for his museum."

Thure Kumlien at the moment was skinning a scarlet tanager. In such a hunting community as that around Busseyville, the ornithologist seldom had use for his small-bore rifle. He disliked killing birds and animals despite the fact that, as he would say, they were thus preserved for generations that might never see the living species. The naturalist worked swiftly and deftly on the small scarlet bird with its dramatically black wings, never loosening a feather in the process. The operation was as precise as that of a surgeon. With similar scalpel, this taxidermist was removing the fragile skin in a single piece.

"You see, Robbie, I do not injure so much as an eyelid."

"I wish I could skin birds like that!"

"You will, one of these days."

"They look so alive when you mount them that I expect them to start singing."

"I hope they will last for many years."

Thure Kumlien was a self-taught ornithologist and taxidermist. There were no professors in either subject at his university in Sweden. To furnish a form over which to stretch his bird skins, he had in his youth tried straw, which proved too bulky and unmanageable. He next tried clay, and in the process he became something of a sculptor. From clay he moved to soft woods, carving the birds, over which he fitted the skin. Finally he settled on cedar excelsior, sewn into shape with strong thread and strengthened at vital points with wire. The fragrant red cedar discouraged insects, as did the arsenic, mixed with corn meal, a preparation with which he carefully removed any fat clinging to the inner surface of the skin.

Having taken exact measurements of the bird when freshly killed, he could, with almost microscopic stitches, sew and stretch the cured and pliable skin over the carefully fashioned form. The final product was a bird which looked indeed as though it might break into song. A modern taxidermist might think Kumlien's methods slightly crude. But many of his mounted birds, still treasured at institutions of higher learning in Wisconsin, look nearly as vibrant as when they first were mounted by Kumlien one hundred years ago.

"How much do you want for your osprey, Robbie?"

"You decide."

"What would you say to fifty cents?"

"A whole half dollar!" Robbie was ecstatic. "That will buy me a day, from dawn till dark. Did you know that I'm buying time from my father?"

"So your mother told my wife."

"I'll certainly need that extra day," Robbie said. "I've looked everywhere, but I haven't even found the whelping den yet."

"I guess Bubs beat you to it."

Zeke Mooney, the fur trader, had overheard Robbie's last remark. He had walked into the foreyard so quietly that neither Kumlien nor Robbie had been aware of his approach.

"That's rotten luck," Robbie wailed. "I just can't believe it."

"You'd better believe it," Zeke Mooney insisted. "We'll show you their pelts tomorrow. Howdy, Professor!"

"Hello, Zeke. What brings you here?"

"To get right down to business," said the man with the noiseless tread, "I want to buy some arsenic."

"Arsenic?"

"That's what I asked for. You've got some, ain't you?"

"Just a little to cure and clean my bird skins."

"Don't matter what you use it for. Just so it's deadly poison."

"And why do you need arsenic?" Kumlien queried.

"To kill that she-wolf so we won't have to fight her in the den."

Robbie began shaking his head slowly from side to side.

"What did this wolf do to you?" the Professor asked.

"Done plenty, the old devil. Kilt my pig, that's what! She'll come back for the rest of the carcass tonight. I'm a goin' to season up that pork with a bit of arsenic."

"I've never believed in poisoning carcasses," Kumlien said.

"Whatcha got agin' it?"

"It also endangers skunks, mink, foxes, badgers, raccoons. . . ."

"All varmints, ain't they?"

"Also local cats and dogs."

"Glad you reminded me," Zeke said, "I'll chain up Tige tonight."

"Also it might destroy blue jays, chickadees, nuthatches, woodpeckers. . . ."

"All useless, no-account critters."

"I have my own definition of useless, no-account critters."

"Don't get your dander up, Professor. Don't matter

one way or the other about the arsenic. Bubs knows where the den is. First thing tomorrow morning we're going to dig 'em out, knock 'em on the head and collect the bounty."

"You won't dig them out if they're in my woods," Kumlien said, coldly.

"They ain't on your land. They're out on Skavilain's Point . . . Dad cuss it! I promised Bubs I wouldn't tell nobody, least of all Robbie Trent."

"We'll be there bright and early, won't we, Professor?" Robbie said.

"We certainly will," Kumlien said.

"Thanks for telling us where the den is!" Robbie shouted after the retreating fur buyer.

4: Into the Wolf Den

Two hours before dawn, Robbie was out of bed and dressed. He tiptoed down the steep stairs and noiselessly awoke his father. Ezra was equally silent as they ate a hurried breakfast including wide wedges of apple pie and big mugs of milk. Robbie found it delightful to be involved in this small conspiracy with his father. His mother had called the whole expedition "a fool's errand, and a dangerous one." They had no desire to wake her.

In the barn, lighted only by the kerosene lantern, Ezra threw down hay for the animals while Robbie milked Brown Bet. The boy did not forget to pour a pint or two of the rich milk into the pan for the cats and into the dish beside Old Tessie, who had lost her most recent litter of pups.

"Poor old girl," Robbie sympathized, stroking the tired dog. Tessie thumped her tail by way of gratitude.

They took the milk to the springhouse, then started down the path which approached the stile. Each had a shovel over his shoulder. Robbie also carried the lantern to light their way. It bobbed along through the vast, enveloping darkness. Their shadows were gigantic and somehow menacing.

Thure Kumlien had seen the lantern light advancing through the woods. He was ready to join them when his neighbors reached his foreyard gate.

"I left Margretta sleeping," Kumlien said softly, as he quietly closed his gate.

"Ellen likewise," Ezra murmured.

As they walked softly along the forest trail, Robbie was wide awake and thinking keenly about the difficulties of explaining to his father the special nature of this "wolfing party." He still had revealed to no one but Kumlien the fact that he was passionately determined to raise a wolfling as a pet.

When they reached the tip of Skavilain's Point, Bubs and his father were already digging. The predawn light was pink and gold as it streamed from the east across the wide lake where noisy gulls were already skimming the water in search of breakfast.

"Man or boy, first one who reaches 'em gets half the bounty," Zeke Mooney said. "Bubs gets the other half."

"By rights, Paw, I should get all the money," Bubs said. "I found the den."

"But you ain't dug more than fifty shovels of dirt."

"I'm tuckered, Paw."

"You ain't tuckered. You're plain lazy. . . . Want to spell us off, Ezra?"

Robbie was proud to see how easily and efficiently his father drove the shovel into the earth and tossed it back over his shoulder. With their fresh energy the Trents were making much better progress. It was a great joy to work beside his father on such an exciting project. The den entered the hillside almost horizontally, and Robbie was determined to dig to the other side of the hill to get his wolfling. Suddenly, however, the excavating became much more difficult. In another moment their shovels had hit solid limestone. Nevertheless the tunnel continued. Apparently it was a narrow cave whose entrance had been covered by some ancient earth slide.

"Wears you down, don't it?" Mooney queried with mock sympathy.

"Can't shovel through solid limestone," Ezra said.

"Maybe we can smoke 'em out," Mooney suggested. "And when that she-wolf comes snarling out, I'll blast her with both barrels of my double-barreled ten gauge."

"I'll bet your Paw can't hit the broadside of a barn," Robbie said quietly to Bubs.

And that was what started it.

"Hear that, Paw? You can't hit the broadside of a barn!"

"Who said?"

"Robbie Trent."

"Whup him, Bubs."

As the two boys circled each other warily, hearts thumping, fists clenched until their fingernails dug into the palms of their hands, other wolfers began drifting in. News of the den had traveled swiftly on the rural grapevine. Ephraim Bussey, the storekeeper, arrived with a seventy-five-foot coil of rope. The Slaggs, the Ladds and the Cunninghams came by way of the beach, carrying guns and shovels. Old, silver-haired Eric Skavilain—with his pert granddaughter, Ingeborg—soon appeared.

Robbie and Bubs had both been watching their twelve-year-old classmate during the school year. The impending fracas became much more determined as she joined the onlookers. Robbie and Bubs had tangled several times. By the standards of the young community, no one could interfere with a fair fight between well-matched boys.

"I'll knock your block off," Bubs said.

"I'll wreck your shanty."

"I could lick you with one hand tied behind my back."

"You and who else?"

"No ear-chawin' and no eye-gougin'," Bubs warned.

"I'm no river rat."

"Call me a river rat and I'll . . ."

But everyone, including the contestants, forgot the fight when Ephraim Bussey shouted, "I just seen the she-wolf! Green eyes, white fangs and all! She's in there, I tell you. She's a big one and a mean one."

Caves in this part of Wisconsin are seldom as extensive as they are in Kentucky and Missouri. Often they are so narrow that only an animal or a small boy can crawl along the tunnel. Thousands of years of trickling water had dissolved and eroded the Ordovician limestone until a passageway averaging two feet in diameter pierced the escarpment. The morning sun, just above the horizon, was in the proper position to send a beam of light down the first twenty feet of the cave, all adazzle with calcite crystals. It was by this light that Ephraim Bussey had glimpsed the mother wolf.

"Only way is to smoke 'em out," Mooney repeated.

"Which is obviously impossible," Kumlien countered.

He lit a sulphur match and held it at the cave entrance. The downdraft of cold air blew out the flame.

The wolfers were frustrated.

"I know a way to settle your ruckus," old Skavilain suggested. "Which one of you lads has the gumption to slide down that hole and drag out the wolves?"

Robbie and Bubs looked at each other speculatively. Both wanted the whelps, but for entirely different reasons. The thought of crawling down that narrow tunnel of rock to face the fierce and protective mother wolf had them both petrified.

"My paw sent me down once," Eric Skavilain said. "Tied a rope to my leg."

"Same reason I brought a rope," Bussey explained.

"I'd go if I was a boy," Ingeborg said, flaunting her pigtails.

"How about it, Bubs?" his father asked.

"I ain't that crazy," Bubs said.

Robbie Trent, whose temples were pulsing, and whose chest was so tight he could scarcely breathe, heard himself making an incredible bargain:

"I'll do it. I'll crawl into the den, if you'll all promise one thing."

"Promise what?"

"Cross your hearts and swear on the Bible that I can have the pick of the litter."

"Agreed," they all shouted, laughing loudly.

(A little later some of the sheep raisers, particularly Ezra Trent, wondered just what they had promised.)

When he saw that his son was serious, Ezra Trent tried to dissuade him from going into the cave. Thure Kumlien reasoned with him. Ingeborg Skavilain protested almost tearfully that she was only teasing.

"Please, Robbie, don't go in there!"

"A deal is a deal," Robbie said grimly. He took the lantern, making sure that he had enough kerosene. He belted on the best sheath knife he was offered. Then Ephraim tied the rope to his right ankle and Robbie crawled into the cave.

For the first twenty feet the going was easy and the tunnel well-lighted. The sandy floor showed many tracks of Old Three Toes. For just a moment the boy felt remorse for the mother wolf.

Twenty-five feet beyond the entrance, the passageway angled sharply, and now Robbie was grateful for his lantern. It shone upon a few stalactites hanging like icicles from the low roof. Already the boy began to feel the chill and the loneliness of the cave. The voices from outside were fading into silence. He was alone in some ancient world, facing what may have been man's first enemy.

To the men outside, the scene was mostly a cheerful one. Wild crab apples had exploded into rosy bloom. Bee-filled clover dappled the grass. The lake was alive with mallards, canvasback, and blue- and green-winged teal, as well as stately white swans and Canada geese. Many of the mated birds were performing, with minute precision, their courting ceremonies, bowing and curtsying, playing elaborate games of follow-the-leader in their nuptial flights.

The men, too, were carrying out the primitive immemorial rites of wolfing, popular in one form or another for several thousand years. Some of them passed the jug, or offered each other a "chaw" of tobacco.

Kumlien and Trent were soon deep in a serious conversation. As usual, it concerned Robbie and his future.

"I say *eight* years in school is plenty and *more than plenty*," Ezra Trent insisted.

"Not nearly enough," Kumlien said.

"But he's read all of the McGuffey *Readers,* part of the Bible, Fox's *Book of Martyrs,* and I don't know what all."

"He needs languages, sciences, the liberal arts."

"They won't help him one little bit to plow and cultivate and harvest."

"Maybe he doesn't want to plow all his life."

"What's good enough for me is good enough for Robbie."

Suddenly they both remembered where Robbie was at that moment. They hurried to the cave entrance where Bussey had just payed out his last yard of rope. The storekeeper waited a few minutes before giving three quick tugs, which was the prearranged signal.

When Robbie felt the three tugs and knew he had literally reached the end of his rope—all seventy-five feet of it—he seriously thought of giving the distress signal and making an inglorious retreat. But his longing for a wolf whelp, and his realization of the scornful amusement with which he would be greeted if he were dragged out, feet first, reinforced his determination to crawl further into the cave.

In the several pockets of his overalls he kept an assortment of treasures, including the stub of a pencil and a tattered notebook. He tore a lined sheet from his notebook and by the smoky light of the lantern printed the following message:

> ROPE TOO SHORT. DEN GOES DEEPER. MUST GET WOLF
> PUP. DON'T WORRY.
>
>   ROBBIE

He unfastened the knot at his ankle, frayed the end of the rope, and tied the note on, butterfly fashion. Only *then* did he give the three-tug answering signal. He could well imagine the general consternation as Ephraim Bussey swiftly retrieved the rope, which obviously was not attached to a boy.

To Robbie this was high adventure. Even the appearance of bats sailing past him in the dim lantern light did not trouble him too greatly. He knew that these little insectivores were harmless creatures who, through some "sixth sense," seldom blundered into any object even when flying in complete darkness.

Cool, fresh air from some remote source kept the lantern burning and gave him hope as he struggled on. But upon turning a sharp corner of the tunnel, he felt himself tumbling and sliding down a very steep slope. As the lantern flew from his hand, he heard a crash and a splash. Then came total darkness. Almost simultaneously he landed in a shallow, icy, underground stream.

His first thought was: "Golly, Paw will be mad. That was our best lantern."

He realized that his situation was now actually dangerous. Even if he could find the lantern, its wick would be wet and its chimney broken. The sulphur matches (like everything else in his hip pocket) were soaked and therefore useless.

Robbie managed to cross the little stream and began climbing the slope beyond. By touching the walls of the tunnel he was able to follow its curve upward. He had not completely lost his sense of time or direction. He believed that he had been in the cave almost an hour and that the passageway had transcribed a rough half circle. Another fifteen minutes of scrambling in the utter darkness proved both of his theories to be right. With a cry of joy he perceived, far up ahead, a faint and oblique shaft of light. He had entered with the dawn illuminating his westward penetration of the limestone escarpment. Now he was reaching a higher entrance, again illumined by the sun.

But this welcome ray of light, toward which he was crawling at top speed, also revealed the snarling mother wolf, her slanting eyes as green as emeralds. Robbie tested the quick availability of his sheath knife, paused for a few moments to assemble his strength and courage, and then with a yell of defiance, crawled swiftly toward the shaggy creature. Maybe wolves do not bite human beings without provocation. But it suddenly occurred to Robbie that he was giving the she-wolf plenty of provocation. She had every right and reason to defend her whelps.

When Robbie was within thirty feet of Old Three Toes, she made her decision. From a hollow, as yet hidden from the boy, she picked up a whelp by the nape of the neck, much as a mother cat picks up a kitten, and raced up the gentle incline to the higher exit. She looked back only once, then disappeared into the dense hazel brush which Robbie knew clothed this entire promontory. Robbie could make an intelligent guess as to her next move. All this area was filled with scrub or heavy forest. She could reach the hollow log on Kumlien's place without once being seen on cleared land. She certainly had other hide-outs (such as the one on the island in the tamarack swamp) where she could lie low until the whelp was big enough to follow her still farther north into real wilderness. In any case, the mother wolf was never again seen by any person in this region.

But what about Robbie's "pick of the litter"? He hastened forward and found, curled in the smooth depression, his heart's desire. Apparently only two pups had been born to Old Three Toes. This twin, who had been left behind, was a silky, golden little thing weighing less than a pound. His eyes were not yet open. He was as clean as a well-tended kitten and as harmless. Wolves are excellent mothers, and Three Toes had been no exception. With her big rough tongue she had kept him immaculate. Robbie was amazed to find that his little wolf was short-nosed and chubby. Only later did he learn that all wolves are born looking much like this one.

The ray of sunlight falling through the upper entrance now touched upon the tawny, deep-furred wolfling as though he were enhaloed. But at this moment the wolf puppy, groping for its mother or for its den mate, suddenly realized that it was alone and began to whimper piteously. Robbie cupped his new and precious possession in his two hands and felt, for the first time, the throbbing life of the small creature.

"You sure don't look like a wolf," Robbie said tenderly, "but I'm going to call you 'Wolf.' And I'm real fond of you, no matter what you look like."

The upper parts of Robbie's shirt and the bib of his

overalls had not been soaked by his tumble into the shallow stream. They now made a comfortable cradle for Wolf, who soon fell asleep in his new nest.

Very carefully Robbie now crawled to the upper entrance and out into the morning sunshine.

"Thank you kindly," he said, looking upward.

A few feet from where he emerged there was a slight opening in the hazel brush. From this vantage point Robbie could see the wolfers below. When he shouted, they all looked up. A great cheer arose from at least twenty throats.

He made his way down the steep and rocky hill, watching carefully to see that Wolf was not bruised in the descent. The excited wolfers gathered around him.

"Did you kill the she-wolf?"

"Where are the pups?"

"Weren't you scared?"

"Where's our lantern, Robbie?"

Dozens of questions were thrown at him, and Robbie answered them as well as he could. But he told them nothing about Old Three Toes, or the twin she had taken with her. He wanted them to have a good head start and a fair chance to survive.

Slowly and carefully he brought out the little wolf.

"Is that the pick of the litter?"

"It's not only the *pick* of the litter, it *is* the litter." He thought that he might be forgiven for this small white lie.

"When you goin' to knock him on the head?" Bubs asked.

"I'm never going to knock him on the head," Robbie said, examining the perfect little ears. "I'm going to raise him to be the finest wolf in Wisconsin."

"Not a *wolf*—he's a *wolf-dog*," Kumlien reminded him. "With Ring for a father and Three Toes for a mother, you've got a very special animal there, Robbie."

"You mean you're going to raise that creature on our farm?" Ezra asked in alarm and amazement.

"You made me a deal," Robbie said. "You, and everybody else, said I could have the pick of the litter."

"A deal is a deal," half a dozen of the men agreed.

"By rights he's mine," Bubs said sullenly. "I found the den."

"By rights he's *mine*," Inga said. "That den is on *our* farm."

Robbie expected Bubs to give him trouble, but he was absolutely dumbfounded to hear such words from Inga. There was mischief in her eyes, however.

"Inga's maw's scared of almost everything. She wouldn't let her have a *wolf* pup," Ingeborg's grandfather said, comfortingly, to Robbie.

"Well," Inga said, "he's at least half mine. But I guess I'll let Robbie keep his half and my half at his place."

Bubs didn't know what to say. He had a feeling that he had been outmaneuvered. And Ezra, in his chagrin, felt much the same.

"I'll let you raise him," Ezra said sternly, "but the first farm animal he kills, you gotta shoot him, Robbie."

"He's not going to kill any of our creatures," Robbie said. But no one there, including Robbie, believed that you can train a wolf to act like a lamb.

5: Wolf's First Summer

Ellen saw them silhouetted against the sky as they mounted the stile. She felt the warm reassurance for which she hungered after a few hours of separation.

Her morning, as usual, had been a busy one. Since it was Tuesday it was ironing day. She had captured the sheets from the wind where they were blowing outward from the line. She put the fresh-smelling washing into the woven willow basket. The stove was lit to heat the irons, so it only made sense to open a jar of her cherries and bake a pie.

Robbie seemed to be holding a precious something close to him. Another kitten, perhaps (as though they did not have enough cats on the place). But as she stepped from the cabin door to greet them, she realized that Robbie was much too excited to be bringing a mere kitten.

Ezra looked troubled, Robbie jubilant as they entered the foreyard.

"Whatever have you found?"

"A wolf, Mom!"

"Are you daft?" Ellen asked. "Let me see!"

"He hasn't even opened his eyes," Robbie said.

"I say we should destroy him right now," Ezra said, "but I made a covenant with the boy."

"What covenant?" Ellen asked.

"Paw said, and everybody said, if I crawled into the den I could have the pick of the litter."

"Did you let this boy go into the wolf den?"

"Well, you see, it was his idea!"

"I see," Ellen said. "I see that you both should have your heads examined."

"It was dark and cold and scary in there," Robbie said. "I really earned this puppy."

"And broke our best lantern," Ezra added.

"But I'll pay for that, Paw."

"Well, thank heaven you are both safe," Ellen said. She held out her hands. "Let me hold him for a minute. He doesn't look very dangerous."

"Trouble is, he'll grow up to be a very large, fierce animal," Ezra said.

"Large and gentle," Robbie insisted.

"Look, he's hungry. He's trying to nurse on my little finger. We'll have to feed him on a bottle."

"I've got a better idea than that," Robbie said. "Old Tessie . . ."

"Of course," Ellen agreed. "Tessie is simply miserable with all that milk."

"Enough for the whole litter that died," Robbie added.

"Well, a covenant is a covenant," Ezra said gloomily. "But if that wolf-dog ever kills so much as a chicken . . ."

"I know, Paw. But he's not going to kill a single farm animal. As Professor Kumlien says . . ."

"I wish you would stop quoting Kumlien," Ezra grumbled. "He's putting a lot of queer ideas into your head."

Robbie retrieved Wolf from his mother's arms and hurried toward the barn, with Ezra and Ellen following. Old Tessie looked up from where she was lying patiently on the fresh straw in a box stall. She thumped her tail in affectionate greeting, then became very excited when Robbie gave her the wolfling. She wondered where this pup had come from and sniffed it critically. Not one of *hers,* she decided, but a puppy anxious to nurse. And Old Tessie knew instinctively that *she* needed to be nursed. She licked the little wolf-dog and pulled it to her with one paw, then lay back blissfully as the small creature found one of her swollen dugs and began sucking avidly.

"Well, that settles one of our problems," Ellen said.

"For the time being," Ezra conceded.

"You two must be famished," Ellen said, "I've got chicken and dumplings and a fresh cherry pie."

Having a puppy named "Wolf" for a pet solved Robbie's most pressing problem. But it didn't solve any problem at all for Ezra. Corn must be planted, tobacco seedlings set out and soon it would be haying time. The Trents needed help. And so it was with a sigh of relief that they greeted a westward wandering ex-soldier who came up the road one day.

A Chicago boy, who had marched and fought for three years for a total reimbursement of thirteen dollars a month, considered the twenty dollars that Ellen offered more than adequate. He seemed a trifle puzzled that the *woman* rather than the *man* made the deal. But being an inward-looking person who offered few confidences, he asked none.

"You'll sleep over here in what we call the out-cabin," Ellen said briskly, leading the way through the pleasant gallery between the cabins. "And if you'll just give me the dirty clothes you have in that bundle, I'll have them clean by tomorrow."

"Thank you kindly, ma'am."

"My name is Ellen, my husband's name is Ezra and this is Robbie. Now what shall we call you?"

"Dan."

"Dan what?"

"Just plain Dan."

At supper that evening it was clear that he liked Ellen's fried ham and pie. He asked for seconds which Ellen cheerfully served, but otherwise he said scarcely a word.

When Robbie went to the barn and returned with Wolf in his arms, however, his face softened.

"What you got there, boy?"

"A wolf pup, half wolf anyhow."

"Say, that's really something. I had a red fox kit once."

"What happened to him?" Robbie asked.

"Folks wouldn't let me keep him."

"Then you *do* have a family?" Ezra inquired.

"No," Dan said, "not any more. Now if you'll excuse me, ma'am!"

He did not light his pipe until he had stepped into the foreyard in the amber light, leaning against the fence and gazing westward.

Later when Wolf had been taken back to Old Tessie, and all had gone to bed, Ellen asked, "What do you think of him, Ezra?"

"You seem to do the hiring and firing around here."

"Well, at least he's quiet and polite."

"If he works the way he eats, we've got a good hired man."

"He was gentle with Robbie and Wolf."

"Any help's welcome in a busy season."

"Good night, Ezra."

"Good night, Ellen."

Robbie and Dan now did most of the chores, with Ezra hitching his dapple grays for an even earlier start in the fields. While Dan was still milking Brown Bet on the third morning after his arrival, Robbie called, "Quick, Dan, come and see."

Dan complied, and for the first time since his arrival, he smiled.

"Trying to open his eyes?"

"Why, they're sky blue!" Robbie said with astonishment.

"So they are."

"I thought wolves' eyes were always green! Old Three Toes' were."

"Maybe they'll turn green later."

The little wolf-dog tried to focus. He saw Robbie, Old Tessie and Dan in that order. And in that order they were his family. These were to be loved and trusted without question. Others would be added to his pack, but only after serious thought. Next day he had little trouble accepting Ellen, but showed a trace of fear when Ezra tried to pick him up.

"I won't hurt you," Ezra protested. "Not yet, anyhow."

"He knows," Ellen said. "Animals always know."

For a few treasured moments each morning, noon and

evening, and for hours every Sunday, Robbie concentrated on his pet. One day when Wolf was playfully biting Robbie's finger, a tooth as sharp as a needle broke the boy's skin and brought a drop of blood.

"You're getting your baby teeth," Robbie said with delight.

Every development was a great revelation to both the boy and the puppy. Wolf soon found his front paws. He could hardly have missed them, they were so absurdly large. Wolves' front feet, which must serve as snowshoes in the wintertime, are much wider than those of most dogs, and this is evident even in puppyhood. Wolf sucked on these interesting appendages, bit them, reached out to touch Old Tessie, and treaded against her swollen milk glands to make the milk come faster when he nursed. He pulled himself up to a standing position, but frequently tumbled over in the straw.

"Acts like he's drunk," Dan said soberly. "Acts like he's got the collywobbles."

"Look, he's found his back feet," Robbie observed. "Isn't he going to be a fine big wolf-dog?"

"Very big and fierce!"

"Not fierce," Robbie said, "or Paw will make me kill him."

"Paws are sometimes like that. But I think I would have been different if . . ."

"Were you . . . a father?" Robbie ventured, then wished he had not spoken.

"Ever hear of the great Chicago fire?" Dan asked with a new voice that was cold and hard. "Well, don't plague me with any more questions."

It was remarkable how fast the wolfling grew. Tessie's milk, meant to supply a whole litter of puppies, was more than ample for the hungry little wolf-dog. From less than a pound when discovered in the den, the whelp soon doubled in weight.

"You're getting real fat and sassy," Robbie said with contentment as the puppy first discovered, then tried to chase his tail.

"You'll never catch it," Robbie predicted.

Hearing the boy's voice, Wolf looked up and focused on Robbie's face. Then to the surprise of both, he barked.

"Why, you're barking!" Robbie exclaimed. "You're not supposed to bark. You're a wolf. You're supposed to howl like this: awa—oooh—ooh, awa–ooooooooo!"

Wolf tilted his head on one side, cocked his ears, then lifted his muzzle and tried his first howl.

Robbie was entranced. "You can bark *and* howl! I'll bet you're the brightest puppy in the country."

Sooner than Robbie had expected the curious little animal was waddling all over the box stall. At first the six-inch sill which separated the stall from the rest of the stable defeated his best efforts to surmount it. But another day or two improved his climbing ability. He started warily down the walkway behind the gigantic animals whose rear ends towered above him.

Spinney, the spirited but gentle Morgan, turned her head and whinnied softly. The two big dapple grays paid no attention whatsoever. There were always puppies or kittens in the barn, and now there seemed to be another one. Stonewall, the mule, brayed loudly, and frightened the wolfling into a swift retreat behind Robbie, who picked up the small, trembling creature.

"See, you'd better be careful," the boy admonished. "And stay away from Brown Bet. She can kick a pail of milk into the middle of next week."

At mealtimes Robbie brought Wolf into the cabin. And it was beside his chair that the puppy had his first taste of chicken. He was delighted with this savory bit of meat and begged for more.

"Don't try to wean him too soon," Ellen cautioned. "He needs Old Tessie, and Tessie needs him, until her milk stops flowing."

"I can hardly wait for Wolf to grow up," Robbie said.

"He'll grow up all too soon," Ellen said a little sadly.

"And start killing chickens," Ezra added.

Dan's eyes flashed fire, but he held his tongue.

"Were you about to say something, Dan?" Ellen inquired.

The ex-soldier shaped his words carefully. "A boy is a boy only once," he said. "Then overnight he is six feet tall and wearing an army uniform."

"Tell us about some of the battles," Robbie requested. "Were you at Shiloh?"

"Yes, I was at Shiloh. But I don't want to talk about it, Robbie." He folded his gingham napkin and rolled it tightly to place it in his napkin ring. "I hope you will excuse me, ma'am."

After Dan had gone out to smoke his pipe, Ezra said, "Dan's a strange man. I can't quite understand him."

"I think I can," Ellen said.

On a later morning of sun and shower, when the fields were too wet for working, Ingeborg came over with a basket of strawberries.

"I picked them for you myself," she told Ellen.

"That was very kind of you, Inga."

"I did it mostly because I want to see our little wolf."

"Is he half yours?" Ellen asked with surprise.

"Of course, he's half mine. Robbie found him on our farm."

"That seems reasonable," Ellen said.

"Where is that boy?" Inga asked. "He should have brought Wolf to see me a week ago."

Ellen called Robbie, and he came running from the barn with the wolf-dog in his arms. Another shower had commenced. The boy and puppy were bedewed.

"Hello, Inga!"

"Hello, Robbie."

"Want to see the tricks I've taught him?"

"What tricks?"

"That's one of them," Robbie said, as Wolf began trying to untie Inga's shoelaces.

"Wolf's pretty clever," Inga said. "Let me hold him."

After a few minutes of deliberation, Wolf added Inga to the pack, but he didn't like to be held too long and began struggling in her arms.

"Behave yourself," Inga said.

"Don't slap him or he'll bite," Robbie warned.

"You're spoiling him," Inga said, but she put the puppy on the floor. "What other tricks, Robbie?"

"Tug of war is his best one."

Ellen had been braiding clean rags for a rag rug. She had given Robbie a three-foot strip of the multicolored braid for this game that he played with the wolf-dog.

Robbie got down on his hands and knees and put one end of the strip between his teeth and growled. Wolf took the other end of the strip and growled equally fiercely. Robbie pulled just hard enough to let the puppy think it was an even match. Inga and Ellen laughed with delight.

"I hope you are staying for our noon dinner. We can have your strawberries for dessert."

"I wish I could, Mrs. Trent. But you know how my mother is. If I'm gone for two hours she's sure I've drowned."

"I must talk to your mother one of these days," Ellen said. "Is she still having those spells?"

"Worse than ever," Inga said.

"She needs a warm shawl, and I've just knitted a pretty one."

"But you shouldn't, Mrs. Trent. How beautiful."

"I'll show you how to make that pattern someday, Inga."

"It won't be any use," Inga said. "I'm never going to grow up."

"What a wicked idea," Ellen said. "I certainly *am* going to talk to your mother and very *soon*."

Ellen, like so many frontier women, spent hours alone. She was too sensible and sane, however, to succumb to the neurosis popularly known as "cabin fever." For diversion she planted flowers, fed the wild birds, knitted endlessly. But during May and June of this year her most entertaining distraction was watching Wolf. By midmorning, while the men labored in the fields, she was eager for companionship and often went to the stable to bring Wolf to the cabin.

At first he was happy to follow her footsteps from

stove to table, or from cabin to gallery, batting aimlessly with his big front paws. She had to be careful not to step on him as he scrambled. Sometimes he made a puddle and was severely scolded. Ellen did not agree with Robbie about punishment. She yelled at the puppy, struck him lightly with the broom and threw him out the door.

His mournful howls of loneliness soon won him forgiveness. When he was allowed to dash back into the cabin, he was always laughing and merry, never apologetic.

Ellen was amazed to discover how acute his five senses were. He would suddenly look up at the cabin window when Ellen hadn't heard or seen a thing. Often it was a moth fluttering so lightly it had escaped even the notice of the moth-eating birds. He did not like tomatoes but enjoyed strawberries. He would watch intently and chase a tiny ant across the floor. He loved to teethe on the broom handle, and since this was an instrument of punishment, he often growled as he pierced the smooth shaft of hickory with hundreds of minute holes.

As he grew, he became an inveterate petty thief, pilfering anything he could carry, such as the feather duster. The fact that Ellen gave wild chase was more than half the fun, and a tug of war to keep the stolen object made the mischief triply exciting. What he needed, of course, were den mates to furnish sparring partners for a rousing rough and tumble. Lacking them, he invented his own games.

One characteristic that is pure wolf was his dislike of change, and his great caution if any object had been altered since last seen. He apparently had a phenomenal visual and olfactory memory. A chair moved from one side of the room to the other would freeze him in his tracks. Eventually he would creep up upon the "dangerous" object, smell it thoroughly and only then accept the fact that this was not some sort of trap.

When Ellen went out to cultivate her vegetables and flowers, she frequently took Wolf along. He investigated the small pink blossoms of her climbing roses, smelled them with his puppy nose, liked the slightly spicy fragrance and began to bat the spray of blossoms with one uncertain front paw. Two things happened. He got a rose thorn in his paw, and he lost his balance and tumbled over. The thorn hurt, and he could not pull it out. So he sat up and howled.

A wolfling's howl, like the cry of a baby, is a deeply disturbing sound calculated to produce instant mother love and concern. Both Old Tessie and Ellen came running. The foster mother nosed the puppy and licked him all over, but could not find the reason for his misery. Ellen saw Wolf biting at his front paw and removed the thorn. The howling stopped and the exploration continued.

At the dinner table that noon, Robbie asked his mother a dozen questions about Wolf's morning behavior.

"Did you teach him anything, Mom?"

"No, but he taught me an important lesson. Little wolves, like little boys, have to learn everything the hard way."

"Well I'm certainly not a little boy any more," Robbie said. "I cultivated three acres of corn this morning."

"That's a big morning's work," Dan said.

Robbie's look of gratitude as he glanced up at Dan sent a momentary shaft of jealousy into Ezra's heart.

"You could have cultivated four acres if you had really tried," he said. "But three acres isn't too bad for a twelve-year-old."

On the Trent Farm, Copperhead, the old gander, had long been the tyrant of the barnyard. Not only did he dominate his harem of geese and goslings, he considered himself the overlord of the chickens and the ducks as well.

Ganders attack by lowering the head and neck until parallel with the ground, spreading their wings, and rushing the object of their anger, meanwhile hissing their battle cry. When Robbie was a very small boy, Copperhead had chased him from the cabin to the barn, and when he stumbled, had used the ultimate gander weapon. Grabbing a piece of the boy's exposed flesh in his strong beak, the big bird had twisted until Robbie screamed. The boy's leg was black and blue for a week.

The old gander had decided immediately that he did not like the little wolf-dog and was only awaiting his chance to teach him a painful lesson. Wolf looked upon the chickens and other barnyard fowl as playmates. He also learned from the hens how to catch and eat grasshoppers. In fact he was soon competing so successfully for these elusive delicacies that he had been scolded by several of the hens.

One day when a hen caught a grasshopper before Wolf could, he chased the bird and jumped upon her in an attempt to wrest the prize. The hen began squawking loudly. Robbie and Copperhead were within hearing distance. Both came swiftly, but the gander reached the scene first and gave the wolfling an agonizing pinch and twist. Wolf howled, and the hen scrambled away complaining noisily.

"I know it hurts," Robbie told the puppy as he comforted him in his arms. "But for once Copperhead was right, and you've been taught a good lesson. *Never* jump on any chicken or duck or any farm animal, do you *understand?*"

Wolf couldn't understand as many words as he would later learn. But he knew when Robbie was displeased. He reached up and licked the boy's face and hoped he had been forgiven.

As Wolf began to reach adolescence, his nose lengthened, his slant eyes gradually changed from blue to yellow-green, darker guard hairs began to emerge from his soft, woolly underfur and his legs became longer.

"You're beginning to look like a real wolf," Robbie told his pet. "It's about time we took a walk in the woods."

Having asked permission of his father, Robbie set forth one Sunday morning after church. Boy and wolf-dog ran happily down a path through the young corn, crossed the stile and plunged into the fresh and breathing forest.

For all creatures recently brought into this world, the

universe is newly minted. It is as though there never had been grass and flowers before, or water trickling over stones. Old wolves and dogs know all about such things. They do not cower under the shadow of a passing hawk, or cringe at the wing-thunder of an upspringing grouse.

As Robbie and Wolf approached the Kumlien cabin, Ring heard them and came to meet them.

"High time you met your father," the boy said to his pet.

The big black dog barked a greeting.

A wolf father knows his sons and daughters because he lives with his mate and helps bring up their young. Ring had never seen Old Three Toes again after their mating and knew nothing about their twins.

"Don't be afraid. Ring won't hurt you."

After a thorough, mutual besnuffing and much tail wagging, Ring gradually accepted Wolf as a junior playmate and began a game of tag with this new friend. They ran in circles, laughing and barking. The high-pitched yips of the wolf-dog blended in canine cacophony with the deep-voiced baying of his mature mentor.

Suddenly Ring skidded to a stop and began sniffing the ground. Wolf joined him. Obviously this was serious business. The wolf-dog had never before trailed any warm-blooded animal, and was not aware that a cottontail rabbit was hiding in the grass ahead. But his first lesson in hunting began as the rabbit leaped for safety. Wolf followed every zig and zag of the hunted creature, but Ring, with superior skill and knowledge, tried to cut off the quarry before he could reach the safety of the nearest brush pile. Robbie did not scold or try to hamper this chase, so Wolf vaguely realized that hunting rabbits was permissible, while leaping on hens and other barnyard fowl was not.

Fortunately for the rabbit, he reached the brush pile a split second before Ring and several seconds before the excited wolf-dog.

Wolf tried to squeeze into the rabbit runway but with no success. Ring quickly lost interest and lay down to rest while his inexperienced young friend ran around and around the brush pile, yipping wildly.

At a whistle from Robbie, both came to his side.

"We'll come for another visit soon," he promised the panting partners. "Right now it's time to eat. Hear that dinner bell?"

Dan had told them a few episodes of his war experiences, but very few. He had been at the siege of Vicksburg. It had lasted so many weeks that some of the men in blue had become friends with some of the men in gray. Against orders, the boys of both sides crawled out of their trenches to lend tobacco, swap pocketknives, or to show each other pictures of their wives or sweethearts.

"Which was it in your case?" Ellen asked.

"A wife," Dan said, "and a little son."

"I shouldn't ask," Ellen said hesitantly, "but where are they now?"

Dan excused himself and left half his meal on his plate. Two days later, when they were again at table, he answered her question almost as casually as though it had been a polite inquiry about the weather.

"My wife and son died in the Chicago fire."

Ellen held her napkin to her eyes. Robbie, who had become fond of Dan, forgot that he was a grown boy of twelve, "two-thirds of the way to manhood." He went up the steep stairs to the loft, with Wolf following.

When Robbie came down again his mother was clearing the dishes.

"Day after tomorrow is Fourth of July."

"I don't want to go," Robbie said.

"Your father and I feel the same."

"But Dan needs something to help him forget," Robbie said.

"I fear it would only make him remember."

"You mean, 'The rocket's red glare, the bombs bursting in air'?"

"That's exactly what I mean," Ellen said. "That's why we're not going."

"When do you suppose we'll have our next war?"

"Never, pray God, never."

"I would go," Robbie said, "if called."

"I know you would, Robbie. That's why I'm terrified."

To go back a few years, Ellen's late father, when not hunting, fishing or training dogs, had delighted in the rearing of sheep. He had in his day raised excellent Shropshires, Hampshires, Cotswolds and Southdowns. He had bred Rambouillet rams to Lincoln ewes for the fast production of lambs which were ready for market by weaning time. During his final years he was seldom sober enough to care how much accidental crossbreeding went on within his flock.

Upon his death, Ellen sold all but a few of the sheep. These she added to Ezra's crossbreeds to produce what may have been the most oddly assorted flock in southern Wisconsin.

Ezra was slightly exasperated to discover a goodly proportion of black and brown lambs born each spring. Some of them were barefaced, long-nosed individuals. Some were snub-nosed and woolly-headed. Robbie found it vastly exciting to try to predict what any particular lamb would look like. He was wrong quite as often as he was right.

Every spring, Ezra made the same complaint and the same threat. "That crazy flock! When Old Tessie dies, I'm going to sell every animal and get out of the sheep business."

But the faithful dog lived beyond all expectation. And the handsome, healthy, but unpredictable lambs were born each spring and were fattened on grain and pasturage.

This year, as usual, it was Ellen who pointed out that it was time that the sheep were sheared.

"They're uncomfortable, Ezra. They're too hot in all that wool."

"Hardly worth shearing," her husband grumbled. "Black, brown, white. I wouldn't be surprised if a green lamb showed up some spring."

"But it's already July," Ellen protested. "You've never let it go this long before."

"Very well, Ellen. We'll shear them tomorrow."

Robbie couldn't sleep, he was so pleasurably excited by the prospect. He tried counting sheep and they continued through his dreams half the night.

Next morning, after chores and breakfast, Ezra, Dan, Robbie, Old Tessie and the frolicking Wolf started down the lane to the sheep pasture. The Trents were about to perform a pastoral ritual almost as old as mankind. Shepherds watching their flocks by night had come to worship the baby Jesus in the manger. Jesus himself had looked upon his sacred mission as that of a shepherd. Ezra seemed a bit less stern as he led the way to the washing pool in the small creek.

"Go get 'em, Tessie!"

Old though she was, she loped off to bring the sheep from the far corner of the pasture. Wolf, who considered this a new game, bounded after her.

Robbie always found it fascinating to watch the wise old dog handle the sheep. The ram with his great curled horns instinctively resented this challenge to his leadership of the flock. He usually made a few short rushes at Tessie, who stood her ground with cool assurance. For the most part she worked silently, rounding up any stray lamb or ewe, keeping them all moving toward the pool. Later she would hold them in a limited area, cutting out one animal at a time and harrying it with yips and nips into the pool. There the men, knee-deep, washed each struggling creature.

Usually she was able to keep the silly animals from panic by avoiding any startling move. Much of the time she crawled forward on her stomach, forcing her will upon the sheep but so gently and firmly that they scarcely realized that they were being dominated.

Today, however, she had a vexing problem. Wolf was as yet completely untrained. All of the sheep, even the four-month-old lambs, outweighed the gangling wolf-dog. Yet, like many striplings, he considered himself fully worthy of a senior partnership. He was noisy, awkward, bel-

ligerent and cowardly by turns. The ram broke away and chased Wolf all over the pasture. Robbie laughed so hard he slipped and sat down in the pool (which was of a delightful temperature on this hot, sunny day). Dan was entertained and even Ezra smiled.

But to Tessie this was no laughing matter. She knew she must save the overgrown puppy from the ram, get the ram back in the flock, round up all the scattering sheep and once more bring them to the edge of the pool. Her joints were painful with rheumatism. This extra effort made her pant with exertion. When she reached the ram and wolf-dog, she distracted the ram's attention, growled and bared her teeth at the surprised puppy and at long last put all in order again. Wolf's self-assurance returned almost immediately. He was learning about rounding up strays. But when one of the big lambs resisted, he grabbed it by the leg and hung on while it bleated as though it were being slaughtered.

Old Tessie's patience was not unlimited. She took a moment from her other duties to roar at Wolf and to bite him so severely that blood ran from his flank. In no uncertain dog language she told this whelp that he must never again injure a sheep. Wolves and even wolf-dogs are usually intelligent. This puppy was no exception. He got the message.

"Poor Wolf," Robbie sympathized.

"Served him right," Ezra said. "And it may have saved his life. Remember our covenant, Robbie! If that savage creature ever kills a sheep . . ."

"Your father is right," Dan said. "We all have to learn. Sometimes it hurts."

"But he isn't a *savage* creature," Robbie protested. "Wolf is mostly *very gentle.*"

"Gentle or savage, I hope he has mastered his lesson!" Ezra said grimly.

By midmorning all the sheep were washed and in the shearing pen. They would dry rapidly on this warm and windy day. By midafternoon Robbie would be holding each sheep to the ground, while his father with considerable dexterity clipped close, but seldom drew blood. Robbie was very proud of his father's skill in removing the fleece, rolling it back in a single thick mat which came off like a heavy overcoat.

At the noonday meal of spareribs and sauerkraut (both products of the farm), Dan was a little less reticent than usual.

"In a short time I'll probably be moving along."

"We'll miss you," Ellen said.

"We could use you until tobacco harvest," Ezra added.

"Where are you going?" Robbie asked.

"I'm fixing to stake out a homestead. Dakota land, most likely."

"Blizzards, prairie fires and Sioux," Ezra predicted.

"Can't be much worse than the war," Dan reasoned.

"You'll be lonesome," Ellen reminded him. "Why not stay on with us?"

"No thank you, ma'am!"

"You're part of the family," Robbie protested.

"That's the trouble."

"Whatever do you mean?" Ellen asked.

"I don't want," Dan began, then fumbled for the exact words, "I don't want to *lose another family,* ma'am."

He rolled his napkin, excused himself and thus missed the best red raspberry pie Robbie had ever eaten.

6: Thirteenth Birthday

Since the morning he had found the wolfling in the cave, Robbie had been given no vacation in that summer of 1873. It is true that each Sunday was a day of rest. But since it was "sinful" to fish on Sunday, there was no day on which he could go fishing.

At supper he now asked, "Could I buy a whole day, Paw?"

"I can't spare you, Robbie."

"But we've harvested the oats and wheat!"

"Fence to mend, Robbie. Brown Bet got into the corn last night."

"But, Paw," Robbie said sadly. "I've got the half dollar right here in my pocket."

"Why is tomorrow so special?"

"Don't you remember?" Ellen asked her husband.

"It's my thirteenth birthday, and I want to buy the whole enduring day to go fishing with Wolf."

"Why so it is, Robbie. I'd forgotten all about it."

"I hadn't forgotten," Ellen said. "I've knitted you a red scarf and red mittens to wear when you go ice skating next winter."

"Thank you kindly, Mom. If ever I can buy a day to go skating."

Dan could restrain himself no longer. "We fought the Civil War to end slavery."

Ezra bridled. "I'll thank you to stay out of this family affair."

"Dan *is part of the family*," Robbie again insisted.

"*Please!*" Ellen pleaded.

All at the table were suddenly silent, eyes downcast, each immersed in his own tumultuous thoughts. It was Dan who broke the spell and solved the dilemma.

"I was thinking of leaving for the West tomorrow. But I'll stay a week or a month if you'll let the boy go fishing."

"Thank you, Dan," Ellen said, "we really do need you."

"I'm *that* grateful," Robbie said.

"Well, Robbie, take the day and keep your half dollar. Maybe I am a bit too stern, as my father was before me."

"The whole day! Did you hear that, Wolf?"

The adolescent puppy didn't know why his lord and master was suddenly so happy, but it made the wolf-dog happy, too. He pulled Robbie's red bandanna handkerchief from his hip pocket and went dancing around the cabin with the stolen object.

For once neither Ezra nor Ellen scolded the wolfling for his mad antics.

Next morning Robbie awoke before dawn and hurried through his chores. By the time the sun had fully arisen over the lake, he was on his way to Busseyville with a paper sack of lunch, his bamboo fish pole and a can of grasshoppers for bait.

The wheat stood in shocks which looked like small thatched houses all across the grainfield. Robbie shuffled his bare feet forward with each stride as though he were skating. This flattened the stiff stubble and saved his feet from being hurt by the sharp straw. Wolf ranged widely over the field. He was nearly four months old now, a long-legged whelp with surprising grace and agility. On certain days he was moody, with a faraway look and no merriment. But today he was filled with anticipation and affection. Often he returned to Robbie and looked up, laughing with his green slanting eyes and lolling red tongue. The earth was damp with dew. A new-washed fragrance permeated the morning air, and a cool breeze blew from the lake.

Suddenly Wolf stopped with an effortless deceleration, poised for a moment, ears pricked forward, reared and pounced. Robbie did not hear the high-pitched squeak of the meadow mouse as Wolf brought to an end a life which in any case could not expect a much greater duration. Professor Kumlien had taught Robbie a great deal about the life-spans of the various wilderness creatures. This fat grandmother mouse had fulfilled her mission in life. She had been born in this field, had grown to swift maturity, had mated, made her soft nest and given birth to several successive litters. At twelve months of age she was the grandmother of several hundred. If it were not for owls, weasels and other natural enemies, her descendants would soon have taken over every square inch of the planet, leaving no grain of wheat for man or any other animal.

Now she had come to a swift and merciful end.

Wolf did not eat her at once. She was his first warm-blooded kill. He brought her proudly and dropped her at Robbie's feet.

"A birthday present for me?" Robbie asked.

Wolf uttered a happy bark.

Robbie leaned over to pick up the dead mouse, but Wolf put a firm paw upon it and growled.

"Indian giver," Robbie said.

The wolf-dog now took his paw from the little animal and stepped back and barked again. Robbie was puzzled. He had not yet learned the etiquette of accepting gifts from a wolf, nor the rare qualities of lupine generosity. Within the pack, wolves bring food to mates and to puppies of all sizes. But they often emphasize the fact that it *is* a gift.

Robbie again stooped over, and with studied deliberation picked up the still-warm corpse. Wolf barked happily. Robbie's acceptance and *acknowledgment* of the gift doubled his joy and the ritual was complete.

"Thanks a lot," Robbie said, "but *you* can have it." He tossed it toward the great hunter, who ate the mouse in one delicious gulp.

The mouse which might have lived another month or two went to sustain the wolf-dog who might live ten or fifteen years at the most. The boy, whose Biblical allotment was "threescore years and ten," stood watching. He was the only one of the three who gave this comparative mortality so much as a moment's thought.

"Every living thing on this planet has a purpose," Kumlien had said. "Together they make the balanced harmony of the flora and fauna, and in dying furnish food for further life."

"Even wolves?"

"Even wolves," Kumlien had said. "They keep the herds of deer, and the other browsing animals, from becoming so numerous that they would consume all the browse, and eventually starve to death. I intend to write a paper on this subject sometime."

Boy and dog reached and mounted the stile and continued down the path through the cool, deep woods, approaching the Kumlien cabin. Ring came bounding out to meet them.

All three raced to the foreyard gate, with Wolf winning easily. Professor Kumlien was working at his bench beside the door. Just now he was carefully skinning two passenger pigeons for mounting. The breasts of the birds, particularly the male, shimmered like changeable silk with purples and greens and tints of gray and rose.

"Well, Robbie and Wolf, I see you are going fishing."

"It's my thirteenth birthday," Robbie said, "and I was given the whole day; isn't that a fine present? And my mother knit me a red scarf and mittens."

"Tell you what I'll do," Kumlien said, "I'll give you what may be the last two passenger pigeons in the world. These two I am mounting."

"Why, thank you very much," the boy said, "but how can they be the last two? There are hundreds of millions of them migrating overhead every spring and fall."

"Millions now, but there won't be a pair left one hundred years from today."

"How can you possibly predict?" Robbie asked, still incredulous.

"You've seen their nests?"

"Just a few sticks balanced on a limb."

"And how many eggs do they lay?"

"Just two," the bright boy said, "and some of them roll out and smash on the ground."

"And you've seen the terrible slaughter every year. Sulphur tossed on bonfires to kill them by the tens of thousands. Shotguns and dynamite to knock them out of the trees at night. Now they darken the sky, are shipped by the boxcar load to the cities and are even fed to the hogs."

"The last pair of passenger pigeons?" Robbie said thoughtfully and sadly.

"Talk about predators!" Kumlien said. "Wolves kill only to eat. Man kills for the mad, wanton joy of it."

The door of the cabin opened quietly and the long, lank figure of Frithiof appeared, his hair tousled. He held in his hands a sheaf of drawing paper.

"Hello, Robbie! Good morning, Father!"

"Your lamp was alight until almost dawn."

"But here are the new plans."

"For the house?" Robbie asked.

"Ah, that's better," Kumlien said, "all on one floor. Your mother will like that."

"No stairs except to my big attic."

"We could ill afford that country house you drew."

"Of course," Frithiof said. "It was only a dream."

"A dream and a memory," Kumlien agreed.

"From your own watercolor of your birthplace in Sweden."

"My father was a wealthy man; I am a poor one."

"But you are resourceful, Father, and you have three sons."

"And many neighbors," Robbie added. "We'll all help at the house-raising."

"I am poor in worldly goods only," Kumlien said. "You are good boys, both of you. And, Robbie, while you are fishing at the mill do check to see how Chris Skavilain is coming with my white oak flooring."

One of Robbie's favorite books was *The Compleat Angler,* a thumb-worn copy of which he had found on Kumlien's shelf. When the boy discovered in Chapter Nineteen that the River Trent was one of Isaak Walton's fishing streams, he felt a close kinship with the author. Robbie's own name was Trent, and many of his paternal ancestors had lived along this English river.

Southern Wisconsin waters lacked Walton's beloved salmon, and one had to travel northward in that state for good trout fishing. But all the nearby streams, rivers and lakes had black bass, pickerel, walleyed pike, perch, sunfish and bluegills, bullheads, channel catfish, and half a dozen other fighting varieties. Not until the introduction of German carp in 1881 did the fishing and fowling begin to deteriorate.

To be a young fisherman as ardent as Walton himself and to be constantly in sight of blue water was sheer torment. With dogged determination Robbie plowed, cultivated and hoed. But often he envied the ospreys and the otters who had nothing to do from dawn until dark except to fish joyously.

As he approached the deep, dark pool below the dam at Busseyville, the boy was so excited he was trembling. True, it was August—"dog days"—and the poorest fishing month of the summer. Furthermore, his fishing equipment was primitive: a fifteen-foot bamboo pole, the same length of green fishline, a red and green bobber, split buckshot for sinkers and a few fishhooks. But the possibilities were incalculable.

He baited his hook with a grasshopper and waited. An iridescent dragonfly lighted on his bobber, which was a sure omen of good luck. But minutes passed before the bobber started to dip, then suddenly plunged entirely out of sight. *"Now"* Robbie said to himself. He pulled and he missed.

After a five-minute wait with no further action, Wolf grew restless and began exploring the shallows downstream. He tried to clamp his teeth on fish wriggling up the current. They slipped from his grasp. He was having as little success as Robbie, but like the boy was enjoying himself. A blue and white kingfisher, crest uplifted in anger, scolded and fumed. This was *his* stream, and he resented these trespassers.

When at 7:30 Ephraim Bussey emerged from the door of his house next to the store, Robbie knew his luck would improve. Ephraim, who often operated his gristmill personally to save the wages of a miller, would now be lifting the gate of the head race to send water cascading through the flume that powered the overshot water wheel. The agitation would excite the fish.

"Having any luck, Robbie?"

"I had one good bite."

Ephraim lifted the gate and the music of the big water wheel began. The iron axle commenced to clank and groan, and soon the sound of the millstones could be heard from within the mill.

And indeed Robbie's luck did improve. The silver bass began to chase a school of minnows that skittered across the surface (as in Biblical times, the wings of an angel sometimes troubled the waters of the pool named Bethesda).

The bass were in pursuit of shiners. But in their excitement they would strike at almost any bait. Robbie should have used a smaller hook for these one-to-two-pound fish. His bobber was in perpetual motion and he was losing his grasshoppers at an alarming rate. However, he managed to catch half a dozen beauties before the excitement of the fish subsided.

Robbie had brought a burlap sack into which he thrust his catch. It was weighted with a stone, tied shut with a length of twine and fastened securely to a willow root. Here his fish could live and breathe until he started home.

Meanwhile, one hundred yards downstream, Wolf had invented a new game. A startled frog had leaped into the water as he progressed cautiously along the bank. He was not sure about these sleek green creatures. Were they dangerous? Were they good to eat? He would catch and eat one, someday soon. But presently he was satisfied to search in the marsh grass and pounce, just short of the frog. The excitement was to see them jump.

As the morning sun moved slowly up the sky, Robbie and Wolf were relishing their holiday. The air was remarkably clear and cool for an August morning. Water bugs skated across the surface. A muskrat carrying reeds to its den in the far bank made a *V* on the water. Far above, hawks soaring in wide circles slowly mounted a rising current of warm air.

At noon, Ephraim Bussey closed the gate of the head race. The water wheel ceased to turn. Now it was so quiet that Robbie could hear the steam locomotive, seven miles away in Edgerton, whistling for the crossing.

Wolf and Robbie shared the ample picnic lunch which Ellen had fixed. The wolf-dog watched every bite Robbie put into his mouth, and now and then barked to remind his master that he wanted his fair share. They dozed for a while after eating, the boy lying on his back in the grass with his straw hat over his eyes, Wolf lying companionably beside him. Just for today, neither had a care in the world.

Then Ingeborg and her uncle, Big Chris Skavilain, showed up, and the afternoon took on additional interest.

"Hello, Inga!"

"Hello, Robbie!"

"Catching anything, Robbie?"

"Not much," the boy said. "Six silver bass and two bullheads."

"Yust have patience," Big Chris said. He crossed the creek on the footbridge and entered the sawmill. The creek was so low in August that the flow would not operate both mills simultaneously. Ephraim Bussey ran the gristmill in the morning, and his sawyer, Chris Skavilain, ran the sawmill in the afternoon.

"I wish my maw would let me fish."

"Why won't she?"

"Afraid I'll fall in."

Robbie suppressed the question he had long wanted to ask. He knew that something dark and unspoken troubled Inga. She was almost as moody as Wolf; all sunshine and mischief at one moment, then sad, with a troubled expression in her eyes.

"Whatcha in Busseyville for?"

"A paper of pins and a spool of thread."

"What's that you're reading?"

"*Old Sleuth.* I swapped."

"Who with?"

"Bubs Mooney. He's got a whole shelf of Beadle's Dime Novels."

Robbie bit his lip and scowled.

"That's rubbish," he said. "Why don't you borrow some good books from the Professor?"

"Like what?"

"Like *Ivanhoe,* maybe. Or *David Copperfield.*"

"Takes too long to read."

"Don't be so lazy-minded."

"You stop lecturing me, Robbie Trent. None of your business what I read. You read dime novels, too."

"Sure I do. I read any book I can get my hands on. I'll read Fox's *Book of Martyrs* or the almanac if there's nothing else around. But I don't *just* read dime novels."

They were silent for a moment. Then they concentrated on Robbie's red and green bobber, which was dancing wildly.

"Pull, Robbie."

"Gotta wait till he really takes the bait."

"Oh, pull, pull!"

"Girls always pull too soon."

Robbie finally pulled and missed.

"There goes my last bait."

"See, smarty, you should have pulled sooner," Ingeborg said, switching her two blonde braids. "I'll bet I could fish better than that."

"All right, Inga. We'll get another helgramite for bait and you can have the pole."

"What's a helgramite?"

"The larval stage of a May fly."

"Robbie, stop sounding like Professor Kumlien. I said what's a helgramite?"

"A soft craw."

"Well why didn't you say so? Where do you find them?"

"Under stones in the rapids."

Inga yanked off her shoes and stockings, pinned up her skirt and petticoat and started into the rapids below the pool. Robbie, already barefoot and with overalls rolled above the knee, leaped in beside her.

"I'd be a regular-born water rat if Mother would let me."

"Why is your mother so dead set against letting you fish or wade or swim?"

"Oh, Robbie," Inga said, stricken, "you know why!"

"I'm sorry," Robbie said. He did know, come to think of it. But it had been half his lifetime ago that the whole community had learned that Inga's tall and brawny young father had drowned. He had gone north for a winter of logging, and a spring of rafting on the Wisconsin River. He had made a false step while booming the logs and had gone under, never to be seen again.

"She's terrified of water."

They were back on dry land again with a can half filled with helgramites. Instead of making Inga bait her own hook as boys often did merely to tease the girls, Robbie gallantly baited the hook himself, and even threw in the line before he handed her the pole.

"Right over there by that log, Inga. Now watch your bobber."

There was an immediate heavy strike and Inga pulled and hooked the fish. Inga's strong arms and her entire body were soon engaged in handling the big fish. Her blue eyes were glistening with excitement and a few drops of dewy perspiration came out on her pretty face.

"Here, Robbie. You take him. He's yours by rights."

"Bring him in yourself, Inga. You hooked him. Bring him in easy, now. Right on that sand bar."

The fish went deep, heading for the pilings under the sawmill.

"Keep him away from those pilings."

"Am I doing all right, Robbie?"

"You're doing just fine."

"I'm afraid I'll lose him."

"No, you won't. Steady, now."

When the great, gleaming black bass came up on the sand bar, Robbie slipped a strong willow withe through his gills as an extra precaution before carrying him to the higher shore.

Inga was dancing in excitement.

"My first fish, my first fish!"

"It's a dandy," Robbie said. "A five-pound bass if it's an ounce."

"Oh, Robbie, see how he gasps. The poor thing fought so hard for life and now he's dying. Shall we put him back?"

"He won't die if I put him in the sack in the water."

"Well, put him in quick. I don't want to see him die."

Robbie put the big fish in with his silver bass and bullheads. The sack flapped for a while.

"Girls really shouldn't fish," he said, feeling a little troubled himself.

The pool was stirring again as the sawmill flume on the far shore agitated the waters. Robbie took the pole and found that the sunfish were biting. He caught and bagged several, each sparkling with rainbow colors. The burlap sack now held enough fish for everyone. And Robbie, who was no "fish hog," put his pole aside.

"How did you get the day off?" Inga asked.

"It's my thirteenth birthday."

"I should have remembered. I'll be thirteen soon. Oh, Robbie!"

"Why do you sound so sad?"

"Let's stay this age forever. Then nothing terrible will ever happen to any of us, you and I and Wolf."

"Wolf!" Robbie suddenly remembered. "Where is that creature? Here, Wolf!" He whistled between his fingers. He had never seen tears in Inga's eyes before.

"I know I'm being foolish," Inga said.

"We have to grow up sometime," Robbie said, "and carry our responsibilities."

"My mother says . . ."

"Can't anyone reason with your mother?"

"Uncle Chris can," Inga said, wiping her eyes with a corner of her calico dress. "Since he came home from the pineries she's a bit more cheerful."

Robbie whistled again for Wolf and from far down the creek there was a faint answering bark. Then in a few minutes they could hear him splashing through water, dashing through the willows.

"Hurry up, Wolf!"

"Coming, coming!" he barked.

"My, what a loud bark," Inga said.

"He weighs nearly forty pounds," Robbie said proudly.

The young wolf-dog, wet and happy, came into an open pasture one hundred yards down the creek. His head was up, his tail streamed beautifully behind him and his shoulder muscles rippled with easy power as he loped into Robbie's arms. He took the boy's cheek and chin gently between his big fangs. Then he kissed Inga, but less ardently.

"Are you happy enough to howl for us?"

Wolf cocked his head on one side.

"Awa . . . oooh . . ." Robbie encouraged.

Wolf lifted his silver muzzle, rounded his mouth and howled his most joyous howl, long, mournful and musical.

Inga knew her mother would soon be concerned, and Robbie realized that even on a holiday he must be home in time for chores. So they and Wolf started homeward through the late afternoon, Inga with a paper of pins and a spool of thread in her brown paper bag, Robbie with his pole and sack of fish.

They found Professor Kumlien drawing a pail of water at his spring.

"How is your wife?" Inga asked. "We all worry about her."

"Thank you, Inga. I worry about her, too."

The girl had an inspiration. "Would Mrs. Kumlien like the very first fish I ever caught?"

"You should keep it for yourself," Kumlien said, admiring the big, gleaming bass.

"But my mother would know I have been fishing."

"Of course, how stupid of me," the Professor said. "Yes, it would make Margretta very happy. We'll eat the flesh of your fine fish. But I will skin it so carefully that I can mount it for you, Inga."

"You mean it will look alive? All glistening like this forever?"

"Forever," Professor Kumlien promised. "Absolutely forever."

He had spent the morning mounting two passenger pigeons for Robbie. Now he would spend the rest of the day mounting Inga's black bass. At this rate he would never lay up for himself treasures upon earth, but many were the treasures he would lay up for himself in heaven where neither moth nor rust doth corrupt, and where thieves do not break through nor steal.

"I'm terribly sorry," Robbie said.

"Sorry for what, son?"

"I was so busy fishing I forgot to ask Big Chris Skavilain about your white oak flooring."

"How could you possibly have remembered," Kumlien asked, "with the fish biting, and with Inga for a companion? I'm drawing a load of logs to Busseyville tomorrow afternoon, and I will ask for myself."

Farther up the trail, where a secondary path turned off toward Skavilain's Point they came upon Bubs and his dog Tige.

"Sic 'em, Tige," Bubs said.

The big white mongrel loved the idea. He came snarling, growling and barking up to the slender half-wolf, who stood nervously, wagging his tail indecisively, eyes averted.

"Call off your dog," Robbie warned, picking up a stout stick.

"Sic 'em, Tige!"

The heavy dog came on with an angry rush, tail held high. He bellowed his fierce hunting cry, the last sound heard by so many neighborhood cats, so many raccoons making a final desperate stand.

"No, no," Inga cried, "call him off, Bubs!"

"Get him, Tige! Kill him!" Bubs shouted.

Tige leaped in for the kill, but Wolf reacted instantaneously. The wolf-dog wheeled and streaked backward down the trail toward the Kumlien cabin.

"He'll murder him," Inga wailed.

"No he won't, Inga. Tige won't be able to catch him."

"You're a horrid boy," Inga shouted at Bubs, "mean, wicked, savage. What has Wolf ever done to you or Tige? Here, take your stinking old dime novel." She threw it at him.

Bubs looked completely unworried. "You'll soon be back for more."

Wolf circled widely through the woods with Tige in hot pursuit and came crashing out of the brush, tail between his legs. But just at this moment Kumlien's Ring had arrived to see what was happening. He rushed in and made a lunge for Tige's throat. There was now an even match between two huge dogs who already had bad blood between them.

"Kill him, Ring!" Inga screamed. "Eat him up, Ring!"

But Robbie and Bubs were both trying to pull the dogs apart.

"Come on home, Tige; we'll get him next time when he's alone," Bubs said.

"Someday," Robbie said, "Wolf will be as big as Tige, and he won't need any help from Ring."

Bubs and his dog started back to the shanty boat. Robbie and Ingeborg patted Ring and praised him. Then they concentrated on the still-trembling Wolf, calming and soothing him.

"But I must get home," Inga said, "Mother will be so worried."

"Good-bye," Robbie said. "Thanks for everything."

"Bye, Robbie!"

Wolf and Robbie sat for several minutes on top of the stile, looking out over the green marshes and the blue lake. From far away a loon called, and Wolf answered with a call equally eerie and wild.

7: The Panic of 1873

When the one-room Busseyville school opened early in October of 1873, Miss Hannah Hitchcock greeted each of the children warmly, then rapped for order, and with little further delay made the following announcement:

"Dear pupils. At this time we usually tell of our summer experiences. But an event of such national importance has just occurred that I think we should postpone until tomorrow our pleasant personal recitals. Now who can tell me the exciting and horrifying event to which I am referring?"

Bubs Mooney waved a grubby hand. "It ain't horrifying. But it's sure exciting. Jesse James and his gang held up the Kansas City Fair and cleaned out the gate receipts—ten thousand dollars!"

"Thank you, Bubs. But that was not what I had in mind."

Robbie raised his hand and was acknowledged.

"Jay Cooke's big bank in New York went broke and started a panic."

"Right, Robbie. Now how will this harm all of us?"

For several moments no one answered. With the single exception of Celeste Henderson's father, no citizen in the township owned a single share of stock. The little bank in Edgerton had not yet closed its doors. In fact that tidal wave had not reached Busseyville, Wisconsin.

"I'm afraid most of you do not read the papers," Miss Hitchcock said reprovingly. "I don't quite understand all of it myself. But I fear we will be facing serious financial trouble in the weeks and months ahead. There may be foreclosures. Already the prices of corn and hogs are down."

Although she was one of the best-informed citizens in the region, Hannah Hitchcock might well have been excused for not immediately understanding what the panic which hit the American economy in September, 1873, might bring.

The Civil War and its aftermath necessitated heavy Federal financing with a flood of paper dollars. These "greenbacks" helped to produce an insecure boom. The building of new railroads permitted stock manipulations which eventually swindled thousands of investors. The city government of New York was incredibly corrupt. So were most of the state governments. President Grant himself was probably an honest man. But influential boodlers around him were robbing the country blind.

The farmers of the Middle West, despite rigged and sometimes ruinous freight rates, were relatively prosperous for the eight years following the Civil War. But in the autumn of 1873 the bubble suddenly burst.

Hannah Hitchcock put all of this as simply as possible. She then asked her pupils if they now understood what was happening. More than half of them shook their heads. High finance was quite beyond them.

"I hope none of you will go hungry or unclothed," she said with real concern.

It was a subdued and troubled straggle of farm children who started homeward that bright October afternoon. Somehow their simple world had been darkly threatened. It was not Hannah Hitchcock's desire to frighten them, but only to instruct them and thus partially prepare them for what might lie ahead.

That evening at supper Robbie asked, "Does anyone hold a mortgage against this farm?"

"Fortunately not," Ellen said.

"But we're in for a tough winter," Ezra predicted.

"You won't be able to afford me," Dan said.

"But where will you find a job and a roof over your head?" Ellen worried.

"I'm an able-bodied man. I'll make out."

"We'll all make out," Ezra said grimly. "We'll all work harder and spend less."

"I'd rather starve than accept charity," Ellen said.

"So would I, Mom."

On the following morning Hannah Hitchcock permitted the children to tell of their summer experiences. Robbie's adventure in the wolf den was applauded by his classmates. The catching of Inga's first fish lost nothing in the retelling. Bubs Mooney had clubbed a wildcat to death, and left out none of the gory details.

Finally Celeste Henderson, in a pretty dress, told of her trip to New York on the steam cars. She said that the fashionably dressed women promenading along Broadway were like bouquets of flowers. The Hendersons had been to the opera and to Niblo's Garden. They had seen August Belmont and other wealthy sportsmen dash by in their glittering carriages. Once at their hotel they were served a fifteen-course meal.

"Which was very silly," Celeste added, "because no one can eat so much food. But Papa tried!"

Everyone laughed because they knew "Papa." Heath Henderson weighed at least 250 pounds. He owned the grain elevator and the farm implement agency in Edgerton. At the present moment he was paying very little for wheat and a mere twenty-five cents a bushel for shelled corn, while still retailing McCormick reapers for $275. Henderson had little control over the prices of grain or of farm implements. But he did earn a commission both ways. This made many farmers angry. To regain some of his rural friendships he had suggested to his wife, Mildred, and their daughter, Celeste, that the whole Busseyville school be invited to an afternoon party at the Henderson country house overlooking Lake Koshkonong.

When Celeste finished her gay recital with a general invitation to a fresh-cider-and-doughnut party on the following Saturday afternoon, almost everyone accepted or said "I'll ask my parents."

The house on its bluff by the lake was not a mansion such as some of those that the Hendersons had seen on the lower Hudson. It was, however, a substantial brick home with several chimneys and a number of gables. The scrollwork was elaborate and fanciful. On the wide front lawn a life-size iron deer lowered his ten-point antlers in defiance of an iron wolf.

All of the classmates who attended Celeste's afternoon party donned their best clothes with the single exception of Bubs Mooney, who wore clean overalls. He was a great deal more comfortable in the games of pom-pom-pullaway, run sheep run, fox and geese, and hide-and-go-seek than the other children, many of whom were afraid to tear or dirty their Sunday-go-to-meeting clothing.

No wrestling was allowed, but there was a good tug of war. The "Wolves" captained by Robbie challenged the "Bucks" captained by Bubs. Sides were chosen. A long manila rope, with a red bandanna handkerchief tied in the middle, was grasped by eight boys on each side. Heath Henderson shot a pistol into the air and the struggle was on. Digging their heels into the green lawn, the strong farm boys, well-conditioned from their summer of field labor, strained and "perspired." (The word "sweat" was not used in polite society, except as it might apply to horses.) In two out of three such contests, Robbie's side won.

The four scholars in seventh grade, Celeste, Ingeborg, Robbie and Bubs, played a spirited game of croquet. Celeste as hostess proclaimed her right to first choice of partner, and she chose Robbie. This left Inga teamed with Bubs.

Inga was not angry with Celeste, but for some reason she was furious with Robbie. At her first opportunity she "sent" Robbie's ball with such a smashing stroke that it sped over the edge of the bluff and down the steep hill to the lake. Robbie went to look for his ball and Inga followed. When they were alone, searching through the marsh grass for the ball, Robbie asked with bewilderment, "Whatever made you do that?"

"You're Celeste's partner, aren't you?"

"But I didn't choose her, she chose me!"

"Serves you right."

"I guess I'll never understand you."

"I guess you never will."

On this golden October afternoon, with the maples crimson, and the sky as blue as the lake, the children of the Busseyville school seemed unaware of the bread lines forming in the cities. Of all his schoolmates only Robbie had begun to ponder the rightness of things.

When he found himself alone with Heath Henderson, watching a great wedge of Canada geese high above them, Robbie asked:

"Why do you pay only twenty-five cents a bushel for shelled corn?"

"Well, Robbie, shipping costs are high."

"But aren't they too high? I read in the *Prairie Farmer* that a bushel of corn shipped from Wisconsin to Liverpool, England, costs seven times as much for freight as the farmer gets at the local elevator. Twenty-five cents plus seven times twenty-five. Why that would be two dollars a bushel in Liverpool."

"And you are forgetting my commission," Heath Henderson said with amusement.

"How much is your commission?"

"That's a trade secret," Henderson said. "But you're a sharp boy, Robbie. If you ever need a job come and see me."

That evening at supper, Ellen wanted to hear every detail of the party.

"Mildred Henderson has never invited me into her home. What does it look like, Robbie?"

"Well, there are red carpets tacked down everywhere."

"With straw under them, I suppose."

"Anyhow they're soft to walk on."

"And does she have horsehair sofas and chairs, with antimacassars to protect the upholstery?"

"Uh-huh. But you should see the wax flowers under a glass dome, and the statuary pieces. She calls one 'The Wounded Soldier' and another 'Courtship in Sleepy Hollow.'"

"What else?" Ellen asked dreamily.

"And a parlor organ, Mom, with ivory keys."

"I had a parlor organ when I was a girl. I think that's what I miss the most." Ellen's voice was remote and sad.

"Henderson can afford all those things," Ezra growled, "because he takes a commission on everything he sells us and every bushel of grain he buys."

"Maybe it's sinful," Ellen sighed, "and maybe it's covetous. But if I could only put my hands on the keys of an organ again."

"I wouldn't want to live in that house," Robbie said.

"Why not, Robbie?"

"Well, Mom, you wouldn't let Wolf come into a mansion like that. And Wolf is worth more to me than all the fancy furniture in the world."

8: Wolf Goes to School

Hannah Hitchcock, whose salary was a meager twenty-five dollars a month, nevertheless "indulged herself" by subscribing to *Harpers Illustrated Weekly*. She shared each issue with the children. Although deceptively brisk for such a warmhearted woman, she made every subject lucid and interesting.

"Remember what we learned last week!" Miss Hitchcock said. "Who is the cartoonist for this journal?"

"Nast," several of the children chorused.

"That's right, Thomas Nast. And what is he most noted for?"

"Lincoln called him his 'finest recruiting agent.' "

"What else?"

"He destroyed the Tweed ring."

"That's right," Miss Hitchcock affirmed. "His cartoon attacks on the notorious politicians of Tammany Hall finally brought them to justice. And how does he symbolize Tammany Hall?"

"As a big, wicked tiger," Inga said.

"Right. And what symbol did he invent for the Republican Party?"

"An elephant."

"And for the Democrats?"

"A donkey."

"Now let's try a little inventing for ourselves," Miss Hitchcock suggested. "Can anyone name another animal that might be used as a symbol?"

Robbie raised his hand and was acknowledged.

"He might draw a wolf," Robbie said, "a brave, deep-furred animal with sharp eyes and ears and a proud flowing tail."

"And what would the wolf symbolize, Robbie?"

"Explorers and frontiersmen," Robbie said. "Men who fight their way through blizzards and hurricanes and floods."

"Also steamboat gamblers," Bubs interrupted, "and river pirates."

"That wasn't exactly what Robbie meant," Miss Hitchcock said.

Robbie had an inspiration. "Miss Hitchcock, may I bring Wolf to school someday?"

"Well . . ." The teacher hesitated.

"Oh, please, Miss Hitchcock," a dozen children pleaded.

"All right, Robbie. If you bring him on a leash."

"Miss Hitchcock, you're the best teacher," Robbie said gratefully.

In preparation for Wolf's first day at school, Robbie read every word he could find in Professor Kumlien's shelf of natural history. He asked the Professor hundreds of questions. He also queried such old-timers as Grandpa Skavilain. Inga came over to help him brush and comb the wolf-dog until he looked like a champion ready for the County Fair.

On the big morning, Robbie and Wolf started for school about ten minutes late. This was at the request of Miss Hitchcock, who thought it would be wise to have all the other children safely in their seats.

Wolf was excited, sensing some new adventure. When a squirrel crossed their path, the adolescent hunter lunged with such strength that Robbie could barely restrain him.

"You'd better behave in school," Robbie warned, "or Miss Hitchcock will give you a good smack with her heavy ruler."

The teacher had advised the children to be perfectly quiet. She appeared calm so as not to frighten her pupils, but inwardly she was terrified. She prided herself on her common sense, and wondered how she could have let Robbie inveigle her into such an addlepated, scatter-brained project.

When Robbie entered, followed by Wolf, who already measured over six feet from tip of nose to tip of tail, Hannah Hitchcock suddenly felt she might faint. But she heard herself saying:

"You see how shy he is. He's probably more afraid of us than we are of him."

Inga's voice helped quiet the trembling animal.

"Nobody's going to hurt you, Wolf," the girl said soothingly. And Wolf, finding this second friend among them, strained at the leash. He pulled Robbie down the aisle to Inga, and gently took her smooth cheek and firm chin between his big fangs.

There were a few "Oooohs" and "Aaahs" from the girls.

"He won't hurt me," Inga said. "That's a wolf kiss. It means I'm a member of his pack."

"Who's afraid of that big faker," Bubs said. He reached from his side of the aisle to tweak one of Wolf's alert ears painfully.

There was a yelp, then a deep-throated growl. Wolf lifted his upper lip in a snarl that showed his two-inch fangs.

"Pull him off, Robbie! Pull him off! He's going to grab me," Bubs whined.

Robbie let Wolf come within six inches of the throat of the cringing boy before speaking sharply and pulling the wolf-dog away to the front of the room.

"Sit," Robbie said, and Wolf sat.

"Play dead." No response.

"Shake hands." Wolf lifted a paw.

"You see," Robbie explained, "you can *tame* a wolf. But it is very hard to completely *train* one. That is why you never see a wolf act in a circus."

"If you think he'll behave, Robbie, you might tell us more."

"He'll behave, Miss Hitchcock. Wolf knows exactly

what I want him to do. But he has a mind of his own. Wolves, unlike dogs, are never wishy-washy. They are often stubborn. There are no stupid wolves, because the stupid ones die young. Professor Kumlien says that the chance of a wolf whelp growing to maturity in the wilderness is so slight that most wolf packs remain at almost the same size, year after year."

"Do wolves kill human beings?" one of the children asked.

"Those are just stories," Robbie insisted.

"How about Little Red Ridinghood's grandmother?"

"That's just a fable."

"Well, how come the state pays bounties?" Bubs wanted to know.

"Because wolves sometimes do kill livestock," Robbie admitted. "But they would be very satisfied to eat wild animals, if hunters didn't slaughter the animals first. Wolves also eat millions of grasshoppers, thousands of field mice, rats and other rodents. Nobody ever gives wolves credit for the good things they do."

"What are some of the other good things?" Miss Hitchcock asked helpfully.

"They are very faithful family creatures," Robbie said. "Professor Kumlien thinks that they mate for life. The male wolf brings the female plenty of food when she is borning the puppies. Then he sits on a nearby hill guarding his mate and his whelps."

"How do you know?" Bubs asked rudely.

"I've asked Grandpa Skavilain and Grandpa Silverwood, and a lot of other old-timers. There used to be packs of wolves around here. And none of the old men or old women was ever bitten by a wolf."

"Do you think that Romulus and Remus really were reared by a wolf?" Miss Hitchcock asked.

"No, I don't," Robbie said, "but I think the Romans told that story to show how courageous Romulus and Remus were, and where they got their fighting qualities."

"You have given us a very interesting talk, Robbie!"

"Can we pet him? Can we pet him? Oh, please, Miss Hitchcock!"

"Do you think it would be safe, Robbie?"

"If my classmates behave, Wolf will."

"Line up silently," Miss Hitchcock said. "Pat him gently, and then return to your seats."

"Isn't he beautiful!" Celeste said.

"He's got real deep fur," Inga agreed.

All thirty-two children, starting with the timid first graders, moved up to Wolf, patted his head or his proud neck and then moved on.

"Wolf is particularly gentle with little children," Robbie explained. "But he sometimes plays rough with me and other big boys."

Even Bubs behaved himself. But Wolf had not forgotten. He growled deep in his throat and snapped his big teeth when Bubs tried to pat him.

"Wolves never forget," Robbie said.

After the communal petting, Miss Hitchcock said, "I think you had better send Wolf home now, Robbie, so we can get on with our other lessons. We had an instructive lecture on wolves today, didn't we, children?"

Robbie went to the exit marked BOYS, which was exactly like the exit marked GIRLS. He unsnapped the leash from Wolf's collar and told him sternly, "Go home, Wolf. Go straight home."

"Will he mind you?" Bubs asked with a trace of anxiety.

"He may or he may not," Robbie said. "Maybe he'll hang around and get you after school."

Bubs did not go out for recess. He was still worrying needlessly when school let out that afternoon. He had decided never again to tweak Wolf's ear.

9: The Parlor Organ

When the grain had been threshed, Dan decided to move westward. He left in the darkness while all the others were asleep. The note, written in script that was almost Spencerian, said simply:

"It is hard to lose my second family. Thank you for everything. Take good care of Robbie and Wolf."

It was signed, "Dan."

For weeks and months afterwards they waited for a letter, but none ever came. Robbie visualized Dan staking out his homestead, building his sod shanty, fighting prairie fires in autumn and blizzards in winter. They had all been slightly surprised to see his copperplate handwriting. It made Robbie try harder to improve his own bold scrawl.

One evening in mid-October when the Trents had finished supper, Ezra pulled his captain's chair nearer the hearth, put on his spectacles and opened the Janesville *Daily Gazette*. The yellow light of the kerosene lamp fell across the page entitled: LIVESTOCK, GRAIN AND PRODUCE. He called to Ellen, who was clearing the dishes from the table in the gallery.

"Says here prices are still dropping."

"Thinking of selling the hogs?"

"Might as well before we have to give them away."

"That's one way of looking at it."

"No use pouring any more corn into 'em."

Robbie, who was sitting on the hearth petting Wolf, looked up with interest.

"When you sell, do we get to go along?"

"Who's 'we'?" his father asked.

"Wolf and I."

"Suppose he runs wild, scares the town half to death?"

"I'll keep him on his leash."

"What do you think, Ellen?"

"Robbie could drive the second wagon."

"I'll do the chores early, and run my trap line before sunup."

"It's a deal," his father said.

Robbie awoke with excitement and dressed by moonlight. Brown Bet was dry at this season, and needed no milking. The boy threw down hay for the livestock and set forth with Wolf to visit his traps.

The moon was setting in the west, and the predawn light was faintly rosy in the east. A skein of Canada geese came honking over Rice Lake, the northernmost of three large ponds marking the western boundary of the Trent farm. A flock of wild mallards floated on water so clear that the ducks seemed to be suspended in thin air.

Trapping was one of the few ways farm boys could make money. To some rural families this extra income was vitally important in this first year of the panic. Robbie and Wolf, "half-tame, half-savage," shared a hunting instinct that had kept both species from extinction. But Robbie, more civilized than his companion, had made one humane decision. He would never again make a "dry set" with a steel trap. The agony endured by foxes, raccoons and other land animals, held by the jaws of steel traps, troubled Robbie's tender heart and haunted his dreams.

Water sets, on the other hand, provided swift and comparatively merciful execution. A muskrat caught in a trap whose chain was staked in deep water, made but one dive, and in a few minutes was drowned. At least that was Robbie's rationalization in those early years when he still trapped muskrats.

Robbie owned eleven clean and well-oiled traps. He set

them very carefully in submerged muskrat burrows in the banks, and on the little mounds of vegetation where the muskrats at night ate lily roots and other marsh delicacies. Sometimes he discovered as many as five drowned muskrats when he ran his trap line in the morning. He took them home in a burlap sack slung over his shoulder.

Wolf watched with interest every step of this operation. He knew that when Robbie skinned the animals, he would be given the toothsome carcasses. On these expeditions Wolf circled the boy by many miles and sometimes caught a rabbit for his breakfast.

Wolf by this time had become a handsome and nearly adult animal. Although he would almost double his present weight, his bone structure was as fully developed as it would ever be. He measured six feet, four inches from nose to tip of tail and stood twenty-eight inches high at the shoulder. His big front paws, which would be so useful for running on a light crust of snow, no longer looked grotesquely disproportioned. He was growing a deep coat of silver and raven fur for the winter, and his pelt was glossy. The soft underfur which kept him warm in any weather was still a creamy tan, but the long guard hairs which extended much farther were dark enough in some lights to make him look almost black. His eyes were jade green and much more slanted than they had appeared to be when he was a puppy. They were sometimes keen and merry, sometimes inquisitive or remote and unfathomable. When angry, he almost closed his eyes and pulled back his lips, showing large white teeth. On occasion he would pick up a tree branch and snap it in two with a single crunch, as he might the leg of a sheep had he not been trained to protect domestic animals. Although he now towered high above her, he still obeyed his foster mother, Old Tessie.

He had a mind and moods of his own, however. On some days he would wander and hunt for hours. Once he was gone for three worrisome days. At other times he clung close to Robbie, the very embodiment of affection, laughing, licking Robbie's hand and eager to play throw-the-stick or tug of war. Sometimes he growled with mock

menace, or "sang" happily in lyrical, long-drawn howls
which terrified strangers. In short, Robbie thought he was
the perfect companion.

Robbie and Wolf found two thoroughly drowned muskrats on Rice Lake, one on Middle Lake and two on
Lotus Lake. They turned homeward, with the sun now a
molten ball above the horizon. Wolf was particularly
happy that morning. Running at a graceful lope, head up,
tail floating majestically behind him, he seemed to be telling the entire world that life is joyous.

And their day had only just begun.

There were nine hogs ready for market. Born in the
early spring and fattened principally on corn and lush
pasturage, they now averaged two hundred pounds
apiece. The five-year-old sow, who tipped the beam at
just over three hundred, was also headed for the livestock
dealer.

Actually, all could have been crowded uncomfortably
into one big wagon. But since Robbie was going along,
both wagons were put into use. Grant and Sherman
pulled the first conveyance driven by Ezra, and the oddly
matched team of Stonewall, the mule, and Spinney, the
Morgan, were hitched to the second.

Robbie and Wolf sat alertly on their spring seat.

"Bet I could beat you to the corner, Paw!"

"No racing, and no hijinks," Ezra said firmly.

Even without a race, the ride through the brisk autumn
air was exhilarating. Grouse whirred up from many a
covert. A flock of canvasback ducks lifted heavily from
Lotus Lake. From Long Hill, Wolf had the first glimpse
of Edgerton, two miles beyond, and far below them. The
cabbage-stack steam locomotive taking on water looked
like a toy. When it whistled, the spurt of white steam in
the cold air was visible long before the arrival of the
piercing sound. White church steeples rose above the
thinning golden elms and scarlet maples.

"Isn't that a fine big town?" Robbie asked Wolf.
"There must be almost five hundred citizens in Edgerton."

Southern Wisconsin had a goodly sprinkling of German-American settlers, most of them amiable and industrious. But neither Ezra nor Robbie liked Hansel Schmidt, the butcher and livestock dealer.

"Purdy goot herd of schvine you got there, Ezra."

"How's the market today?"

"Vell, de market goes oop, and de market goes down."

"Up or down, you make money, don't you, Hans?"

"Schust the same, you gotta be schmart to make money, no?"

"You're 'purty schmart,' Hans."

"Vell, I pet my English is schust as goot as your German?"

"Much better than my German, Hans. How much are you paying?"

"I giff you four cents a pound for de pigs. Three cents for de sow."

"Not enough," Ezra said.

"They should bring five cents," Robbie interrupted. "It says so in the Janesville *Daily Gazette,* doesn't it, Paw?"

"Who asked you, poy?" Schmidt rumbled, then seeing Robbie's big, green-eyed companion, he exploded, *"Gott in Himmel.* Vot's dat? A volf?"

"Howl for Mr. Schmidt," Robbie said.

"Awa—oooh—ooh, awa oooooooooo!" the obedient wolf responded.

"Ya, dat iss a volf, all right. Vot you vant to raise a volf for? Now keep him back, keep him back!" Hans Schmidt held his sharp cattle goad aggressively.

"He's on a leash," Robbie said.

"I tell you vot," said the fat livestock dealer. "I giff you a hundred dollars for all de schvine."

"Make it one hundred and ten dollars."

"One hundred ten in greenpacks!"

"In hard money."

Wolf howled again.

"Ya, in hard money." Hans Schmidt's hands trembled as he turned the lock on his safe. *"Gott in Himmel,* a volf yet."

Wolf's mobile face was a picture of happy puzzlement.

He didn't know why Robbie was laughing, nor why even Ezra for once seemed approving.

Before they mounted their wagons and turned back into Main Street, Ezra said to his son, "I want to use some of this money to buy your mother a present."

"Mom wouldn't want it."

"She looks dead-beat from overwork and worry."

Robbie saw the sadness in his father's face and heard the sorrow in his voice. But he also saw the determined set of his father's jaw.

"But the panic, Paw!"

"There's always some reason!"

They tied their teams in front of Newton's Furniture Emporium on Fulton Street. The usually busy store was almost empty and Newton himself waited upon them. He had the harassed look of all the merchants that autumn.

"I want to buy a nice present for my wife."

"How about a carpet sweeper?"

"No, nothing like that."

"A whatnot with assorted seashells, gilded ones if you like?"

"Something bigger."

"A horsehair sofa?"

Ezra's gaze wandered around the crowded furniture store until his eyes lit on the most beautiful object in the room. It was a walnut Mason and Hamlin parlor organ with inset panels of red velvet and enough fretwork to decorate a stage set in some theater. He knew he couldn't afford it!

"That's a really fine organ," Newton said. "Genuine ivory on the white keys, black keys genuine ebony. Would you like to play it, Mr. Trent?"

Ezra looked at his great calloused fingers, split as were Robbie's at the corner of each nail from cornhusking. In the winter they both left a thin trail of blood behind them on the snow.

"You know I can't play," Ezra said with a subdued ferocity which surprised even Robbie. "Can't play, can't do much of anything except farm, and that doesn't earn us much more than a bare living."

"Paw, you can shear a sheep without ever bringing blood, hew an oak log right to the line—why, you can do a thousand things. Shucks, Paw, you can lift a hundred-pound bag of wheat under each arm, and walk up the ladder to the granary like it ain't nothing."

"Thanks, Robbie. But I can't play an organ. Would you kindly play it for us, Mr. Newton?"

"Glad to," Newton said, "right glad, although I'm not much of an organist myself." He played the "Battle Hymn of the Republic," missing only a few notes.

"What would such a thing cost?" Ezra asked fearfully.

"Well, it was one hundred and seventy-five dollars."

"Might as well forget it," Ezra said.

"But I marked it down to one hundred dollars, since the panic."

"Far beyond my means," Ezra said without hope.

"To tell you the truth," Newton said, "nobody's going to buy a parlor organ in this terrible year. I'll sell it to you for seventy-five dollars. And that's a real bargain. Far below what it cost me."

"What do you think, Robbie?"

"That's more than half our pig money for the whole year," Robbie said. "But I think you should buy it, Paw. It will make Mom happier than anything she ever got in her life."

"We'll take it," Ezra said, feeling both elated and a trifle terrified.

"Shall I have it sent out?"

"Nope. Put it in my wagon behind the dapple grays. I want to see Ellen's face when we drive in today with that parlor organ."

While her men were in Edgerton selling the hogs, Ellen Trent worked diligently in her cabin, washing the few windows and hanging clean curtains, dusting, sweeping, organizing—attending to all the tremendous trivia and hard labor that gave her such pleasure when she was well and happy, and which seemed such dreary drudgery when she was sad and tired.

Although several frosts had killed most of her flowers, the yellow, bronze and red chrysanthemums were still in their prime.

"They grow old gracefully," she told herself as she cut them for her three treasured vases.

There was an important reason for her activity. For the next two weeks it was her turn to "keep" the teacher. Country schoolteachers were admittedly underpaid and overworked. But as a dubious, partial compensation they were given meals and lodging at the houses of the various pupils. The school board arranged this schedule, using common sense in the process. For instance, they did not expect Miss Hitchcock to live in the shanty boat with Bubs and Zeke, and they did expect Mildred Henderson to offer hospitality at least twice during the year. With a big house and servants, it was no real burden to the Hendersons, and it provided two happy fortnights for the teacher.

This year's itinerary directed Hannah to the Trent cabin immediately after her first two weeks with the Hendersons. This made Ellen a trifle uneasy. The contrast between floral wallpaper and hewn-oak interiors, between hand-painted china and plain ironware were but a very few of the differences. Hannah Hitchcock was a sensible woman and a good friend of the Trents, but the Hendersons had a zinc-lined bathtub and the only inside plumbing in the neighborhood.

"At least I have that old mahogany four-poster," Ellen thought. This three-quarter-sized bed was one of the few luxuries that had been retained from her more affluent girlhood. It stood in the out-cabin with tester and flounce crisp and fresh for the occasion. She took from her linen chest her best sheets, sweet with the scent of lavender, and also her Walls of Jericho counterpane.

"Good thing Dan's on his way," Ellen thought with a touch of sadness. "This way I have a guest room. But I'd better cover that empty bunk with my Young Man's Fancy." It was her "second-best" quilt.

"Keeping" the teacher was a worry and a delight for many a cabin-bound woman. It meant conversation with the meals, instead of "victuals" bolted down noisily by hungry men. It meant a breath of the outside world (emanating in this case from a woman who had once been to the Holy Land and had even seen the Egyptian Pyramids). It was laughable how everyone tried to say "isn't" instead of "ain't" when the schoolteacher was with them.

Ellen was so happy she was already singing "Annie Laurie" when Ezra and Robbie drew into the yard with some large object in the first wagon. She ran out to greet them, all excitement and curiosity. And when Ezra untied the binding twine and threw aside the old sheet to reveal the polished walnut, red plush insets, and ivory and ebony keys, she covered her face with her apron and wept.

Ezra jumped down and did something Robbie had seldom seen before. He drew Ellen to his shoulder and put his arm around her.

"There, lass, there, there! We thought to please you."

"Are you daft, Ezra? With the hard times and all!"

He kissed her. And that was a real shock to Robbie. It was the very first time in his life that he had seen his father kiss his mother.

Two days later Hannah Hitchcock arrived with a bulging carpetbag in one hand and a violin case in the other.

"Why, Ellen, we can play duets," she said when she saw the organ.

"I have not entirely forgotten," Ellen said.

"Your organ playing is probably better than my fiddling."

"That I doubt," Ellen said. "But first I must get you settled and comfortable."

"Snug as a bug in a rug," Miss Hitchcock said when she saw the out-cabin. "A hearth laid with firewood. Flowers on my table. And a reading lamp. Who could ask for anything more?"

"It must seem plain after the Hendersons'."

"All those whatnots and gimcracks!" Hannah said. "I was born to simpler fare."

The two weeks went rapidly. Robbie loved and respected his teacher, the more so because she completely accepted Wolf's presence in the house. The volumes which she carried in the carpetbag nearly filled the deep window sill beside the four-poster.

Although Thure Kumlien had many books (his one extravagance), Robbie had never before seen some of Miss Hitchcock's. Parker's *Natural and Experimental Philosophy* was a complete revelation.

"May I read this one, Miss Hitchcock?"

"Any book I have is yours, Robbie."

Natural Philsophy did not concern birds and animals as Robbie had imagined. But it did concern "natural forces" such as wind, falling water, fire and electricity. Here he first heard the magic name, Sir Isaac Newton.

He learned about the largest objects in the universe, the great suns that we call stars, and about the most minute particles called atoms. Could it be possible that the thickness of the wall of a soap bubble is but one two-millionth of an inch? How strange and how wonderful!

He found the chapter on "the recently invented telegraph" to be completely fascinating. Into one of his many notebooks he carefully copied the Morse Code. Now if he were deep in a mine on the Comstock lode and the roof fell in, he would know how to signal for help by tapping on a car rail or a pipe.

Dot, dot, dot; dash, dash, dash; dot, dot, dot. Someone at the pit head would decipher this as SOS.

Robbie kept his lamp alight for extra hours as he turned the pages by Richard Green Parker, who apparently knew everything there was to know about Mechanics, Hydraulics, Acoustics, Optics, Electricity, Astronomy and a dozen other scientific subjects.

Wolf drowsed on his side of the bed, sometimes uttering faint yelps and twitching his muscles as he chased a dream rabbit through his sleep. Occasionally he opened his eyes and blinked at the lamp. Why couldn't Robbie put out the light and go to sleep?

"Good old Wolf. There are a million things I don't know about the universe. And there are a couple of million you don't know, and I'll never be able to tell you."

The faint note of sadness in Robbie's voice reached a part of Wolf's brain more sensitive than its human counterpart, a maze of sensual responses that could interpret the slightest whiff on the wind, that could "hear a cloud passing over," that could know to the finest nuance the exact state of Robbie's sorrow or happiness. He reached over and licked Robbie's hand. Robbie turned down the wick, blew out the lamp and lay for a time, eyes closed, but brain slowly reeling through the Milky Way which the Indians believed was their Happy Hunting Ground and where they and their animals would live in bliss for all eternity.

Fortunately Wolf had been conditioned by degrees to the parlor organ. He had seen it placed in the wagon in Edgerton, seen it unwrapped and carried into the cabin, and had approached it with caution when it had been awarded its place of honor.

True, it was strange and therefore potentially dangerous. But since his family approved, Wolf decided to accept the general verdict. Ellen played a few Methodist hymns softly, and Robbie and Ezra sang to her accompaniment:

> "Yes, we'll gather at the river
> The wonderful, the beautiful river,
> Gather with the saints at the river
> That flows by the throne of God."

Their voices were untrained, but not off key. Singing at Sunday services and Thursday evening prayer meetings had kept them moderately capable of the simpler hymns.

Very rarely had they sung together in their cabin home. But now, with the new organ to inspire them, they found a pleasure that had long been missing.

Wolf listened to the music coming from this strange box with interest and slight apprehension. He held his head at an angle, alert and questioning. But to Robbie's great relief he did not howl.

However, after Hannah Hitchcock arrived, a new sound was added. When she tucked her violin under her chin and began to fiddle, Wolf howled mournfully.

"He's singing with us," Ellen suggested doubtfully.

"He's doing no such thing," Hannah Hitchcock countered. "He's critical of my violin playing."

"I'm ashamed of you," Robbie said, "insulting Miss Hitchcock."

"Throw him out," Ezra ordered.

"Wait a moment," Hannah pleaded. "This is very interesting. Will you play a few chords on the organ, Ellen?"

The gentle theme of "Beulah Land" came from the reeds. Wolf did not howl.

"Now, all together, let's sing one verse!"

> "Oh, Beulah Land, sweet Beulah Land!
> As on thy highest mount I stand,
> I look away across the sea
> Where mansions are prepared for me
> And view the shining glory-shore
> My heav'n, my home for evermore."

Again Wolf was attentive but did not howl.

"You see," Miss Hitchcock said triumphantly, "it's my violin that touches some inner vibration."

While the others listened, Robbie's teacher now ran scales on the violin. When she reached the E above high C, Wolf tipped his muzzle toward the ceiling and howled.

"That's tonight's lesson in canine acoustics," Hannah laughed. "I'll play an octave lower and there will be no howling. This animal is tuned in a certain way. Incidentally, he probably can hear vibrations far above and below the ones that register on the human ear."

On this and subsequent evenings Robbie found it stimulating to have his teacher staying with them. One evening the conversation turned to the plight of the farm communities during these hard months, which threatened to extend into years, of bleak depression.

"It's the grain and cattle dealers," Ezra said with anger.

"It's the merchants. They're downright robbers when it comes to household items," Ellen added.

"I think it's mostly the railroads," their alert son chimed in.

"I agree with all of you," Hannah Hitchcock said, "but I think Robbie has found the real culprit. Discriminatory and outrageous freight rates make beggars of us all."

"But what can we do about it?" Ezra asked in despair.

"We can join the Grange, that's what we can do," Hannah Hitchcock said. "The Patrons of Husbandry, millions strong, can stand up to the railroads."

"I don't hold with secret societies, the Seven Orders, the rituals and all that folderol."

"Very well, Ezra Trent, but you'll thank the Grange for making the state legislators see the light," Hannah Hitchcock contended with spirit. "One of these days there will be regulatory laws concerning freight rates."

"I understand that women can join as full-fledged members," Ellen said wistfully.

"That's another thing I dislike about the Grange," Ezra grumbled.

"Why shouldn't women be treated as equals?" the schoolteacher wanted to know. "When they build the Grange Hall there will be concerts and Redpath lecturers and picnics and parties."

"I think I'm going to join whether you do or not, Ezra!"

There was a sudden silence at the supper table.

"If you will excuse me, please!" Ezra said, rolling his napkin. He only asked to be excused when they were keeping the teacher.

10: The Shanty Boat

Not long after Miss Hitchcock had moved along to her next hostess, a shocking event occurred in Robbie's life.

One November morning when he and Wolf ran the trap line, they discovered that they had been robbed. The eleven careful muskrat sets were as familiar to the wolf-dog as to the boy. The trap line began at the head of Rice Lake where an underwater muskrat hole tunneled into the steep bank. Boy and dog always approached each set with tingling anticipation. Wolf had been taught to stand safely back so that he would never be caught (although such a small trap would not seriously have injured the big and increasingly husky animal). However, with some sixth sense, Wolf invariably knew if there was a muskrat in the steel trap and sometimes barked the news to Robbie. The muskrat would always be drowned, and deep in the water, sometimes hidden under floating weeds or brush. Wolf perceived through some disarrangement of flotsam, or a broken cattail, that a catch had been made. In fact Wolf was so keenly aware of every stick and stone in the mile-long trap line that if the branch of a tree lay across their path where no branch had been before, he stopped and investigated it with the greatest caution.

Wolf therefore knew before Robbie did that something was radically wrong. He sniffed the frosty morning air. He carefully sniffed the footprints of boots other than Robbie's and of big dog tracks that were not his own.

"What's the matter, Wolf? Have some hunter and dog come this way?"

"Rrrr-owww woof."

"Is that so? Who was it?"

Wolf set up a violent bit of barking.

"You know who it was, but you can't tell me?"

"Aaarf."

"You'll be able to talk one of these days."

Wolf looked brightly up at his beloved master and licked his hand. Robbie petted the big, intelligent and silky head roughly and affectionately.

There was no evidence of the trap chain at the first set. Robbie felt carefully with his hickory stick. Next he rolled up the sleeve of his heavy sweater and investigated by plunging his hand and arm into the icy water. No trap, no muskrat, nothing!

"Muskrat might have pulled it loose," Robbie puzzled.

Wolf cocked his head on one side.

"You don't think so, do you, Wolf? And I don't either." They hurried on to the next set.

The muskrat houses which dotted the edge of the lake were conical mounds of marsh vegetation about two feet high. The interiors of these mounds were hollowed out by the muskrats to furnish winter-tight living quarters. When winter rains had soaked this pile, it froze into a solid shelter. The muskrats were at least as warm and snug as Eskimos in their igloos. By common agreement no trapper cut into these mounds or set their traps in them. Men and boys who speared muskrats with long slender rods of iron were considered pillagers. After thrusting the iron into the house, they could feel it if they had impaled the poor animal, and to get the carcass they had to tear apart the house. This practice ruined any muskrat marsh, since it left the whole muskrat family with no safe, warm place to come up for air from beneath the ice. Next season such an invaded marsh had few muskrats.

At Robbie's second set, as at the first, the trap was gone.

"Wolf, we've been robbed!"

The wolf-dog growled fiercely, telling Robbie what he intended to do if they caught the thief. Everywhere the results were the same. All down the shores of Rice, Middle and Lotus lakes, every set had been discovered, and all traps (plus any muskrats they might have contained) were missing.

Robbie and Wolf came sadly home and were only slightly mollified by a good breakfast of hot johnnycake and side meat.

"I slaved and saved for those traps," Robbie said mournfully.

"I know, Robbie." Ellen put her hand sympathetically on his arm.

"I'll bet it was Bubs."

"Now, be just," Ezra warned. "You can't be sure it was young Mooney."

"I'm going to kill him," Robbie threatened.

"Robbie Trent!" his father and mother cried out simultaneously.

"Thou shalt not kill," his father said in his stentorian voice, which could still make Robbie shiver almost as though it were indeed the voice of God.

"Oh, Robbie, Robbie," his mother grieved. "Even to say such a thing is so wicked."

"God could strike you dead," Ezra said. "To think such a thing is as wicked as to do it."

"Well, Cain slew Abel," Robbie said stubbornly.

"Be quiet!" his father said. And Robbie was quiet.

"Maybe this is a sign," Ellen said. "Maybe it means that God does not want you to trap poor little animals."

"It may take me a year, but I'll earn the money and buy some new traps."

But he was not at all sure that he would ever trap again. Somehow all the joy had gone out of the venture. He thought too of the muskrats, most of them still safe in their houses with lily bulbs and roots stored for the winter. It was an unexpected consolation.

Robbie's rage slowly waned. He realized that he had

never seriously intended to kill Bubs. But he was determined to thrash him to within an inch of his life. Young Mooney, however, did not attend school for several days. When he returned he looked pale and ill, and it would not have been fair to fight him in such a weakened condition. Besides Christmas was mellowing everyone. At home and at school there were decorated trees. Ellen played "Silent Night," "Deck the Halls" and all the other stirring old carols. The spirit of the season was working its annual miracle.

Robbie counted the small silver in his sock beneath the mattress. He had less than two dollars, which certainly would not buy the presents he wished to give his mother, his father, Miss Hitchcock, Professor Kumlien, Inga and Wolf.

Robbie realized he must sell his furs, but there was only one fur dealer in many miles. Determined not to let Zeke Mooney swindle him again, he nevertheless headed toward the shanty boat with a sack filled with thirty-nine muskrat skins and four fine, dark mink pelts. For a moment he considered the advisability of taking Wolf with him, but on second thought he realized that his wolf-dog was still twenty pounds under the weight needed to punish Tige.

Still sorrowful concerning the theft of his traps, but excited by the upcoming sale of his autumn catch, he went whistling down the path toward the foot of Lake Koshkonong where the Mooney boat was docked. Here the current of Rock River resumed its swift strength.

Robbie wondered why he felt a yearning that was almost pain every time he saw that shabby old boat. He supposed it was the sense of freedom it offered. Zeke and Bubs could up-anchor and away at any time they desired. During the spring floods, when the water was high over the insignificant dams in the river, they could float all the way to New Orleans if they wished.

There was another advantage. Zeke Mooney had no farm. Except for fattening a pig, in a little pen on "borrowed land," the Mooneys had no labor whatsoever. No horses, no cows, no sheep, no chores, no milking and no forking of manure or throwing down hay. It would be Beulah Land not to plow and harrow and plant all spring, and harvest and plow again all autumn. A boy as free as Bubs should kneel down and thank an all-merciful God that his father did not own a farm.

Another thing. If you had a boat like that you could shoot wild ducks and geese right from the deck without even wetting your feet. You could fish all day and all night if you wished, or leave setlines for big, fighting channel catfish—real monsters here where the river was deep and the current strong.

Living the life of Bubs would be living the life of a prince.

When Robbie reached the gangplank, he shouted, "Mr. Mooney, you got Tige tied up?"

Zeke Mooney came from the cabin so silently he might have been a panther. He could be smooth as cream when he wanted to be.

"Well, Robbie. Come aboard. I presume you have some furs in that gunny sack. Tige is off with Bubs somewhere."

"I figured I would never sell you my furs again," the boy explained, "but I'm giving you one more chance."

"Pay you the top price every time. Same as if you took them all the way to St. Louis."

"That's what you always say!" Robbie exploded. "But last year you cheated me."

"Let bygones be bygones," Zeke said, putting his thumbs under his purple suspenders. "Come in, young man, come in, it's cold out here."

Inside, the cabin was exactly what one might imagine. There was a potbellied stove, the coals glowing through the isinglass. Guns and fishing poles were supported by pegs in the wood paneling. There was a whole shelf of dime novels (which Robbie scorned, but wished he had a chance to read). There was a long wooden table (polished with the grease of many pelts) and a couple of "sittin' chairs." A loaf of bread, half a ham and a jug of whiskey rested on the table.

"Pour you a drink, Mr. Trent?" Zeke winked broadly.

"That's the Devil's own brew. My paw said so."

"Never did me no harm," Zeke said. "How about some bread and ham?"

"Thank you kindly," Robbie replied. "But I'm here to sell my pelts. It won't do you a bit of good to butter me up."

"Furs ain't bringing much, especially this year."

"That's what you told me last year."

"It's the Gospel truth. Furs is way down. Now if you should have a prime black bear in that sack of yours, extra large and extra silky, I might go to eight dollars."

"There hasn't been a bear around here in years."

"How about otters? I'd go as high as five dollars."

"I don't trap otters," Robbie said. "They're so smart and playful."

"You've been letting the Professor addle your wits," Zeke said. "Varmints is jest varmints, put in the world to shoot and trap. How about your Wolf? I'd pay one-fifty. And you could still collect the bounty."

Robbie was horrified. "I wouldn't sell Wolf for one million dollars."

"Well, what do you have in that sack?"

"Thirty-nine muskrats and four dark mink."

"Let's see them, boy! I haven't got all day."

Onto the table Robbie poured the whole of his autumn harvest, perfectly stretched hides, the muskrats cured fur side in, the dark mink, fur side out.

"Pretty ratty bunch you got there," Zeke said.

"They're all prime skins," Robbie said hotly. "I worked hard to trap and skin these furs. My knife never slipped once. There's not a hole in any pelt. No fat on any hide."

"I was just joshing you, boy. Them's pretty fair skins. But big muskrats only bring a dime, kits five cents, mink about a dollar."

"You're trying to rob me again. You and Bubs. You're both robbers."

"Now wait a minute, son; I resent that."

The purr departed and the claws came out. "You know I could thrash you just like I do Bubs. And you could scream and nobody would hear you."

Robbie knew he had been impolite.

"I apologize," he said sullenly.

"Apology accepted, this time," Zeke said. "But what do you mean about Bubs?"

"He stole all my traps."

"You don't say! How could you prove it?"

"They're hanging right over there on the wall," Robbie said. "I saw them when I first stepped in."

"Let's have a look at them, Robbie."

The boy, trembling with indignation, moved toward the traps. "I've got my initials, R.T., scratched on the bottom of every trigger pan."

Zeke lifted each circle—the trigger pans were filed smooth. The rest of the trap was slightly rusted.

"He filed them off," Robbie raged.

Zeke had a mind to hit the boy with the back of his hand. Then he thought better of it.

"I'll tell you what I'll do, Robbie. I'm going to give you the top price of fifteen cents for all your muskrats, big ones, small ones and kits. And I'll pay you one-fifty apiece for your mink. And I'll throw in an extra dollar because it's almost Christmas."

"And how about my traps?"

"Them ain't your traps, son. But I'm going to whip Bubs, like I always do, jest to throw the fear of God into him."

Robbie did some lightning calculating in his head and decided Zeke was also paying for the traps.

"Well, all right," he said grudgingly, "it's a deal. But I'm still curious. Why do you larrup Bubs so much?"

Zeke took a drink from the jug, and scratched his head thoughtfully. "Why do I larrup Bubs? Never gave it much thought. My paw whopped me, and his paw whopped him. I guess it just comes natural in the Mooney family."

"And Bubs kicks his dog."

"Aw, he's gotta have some fun," Zeke said.

"Well, Merry Christmas," Robbie said.

"Merry Christmas, boy. A pleasure to do business with you."

11: The Wolf at the Door

"You and Wolf are about the same age," Thure Kumlien observed, as the Professor, the boy and the wolf-dog progressed down the path toward Busseyville.

"How can that be?" Robbie wondered. "Wolf is only eight months old, and I am thirteen years."

"I mean you are both adolescents," Kumlien explained. "Sometimes Wolf yips like a puppy, and at other times his growl is very deep."

"And *my* voice breaks also," Robbie said.

"Nothing to be ashamed of," the Professor said gently. "You are both progressing nicely. You are growing in mind and body. Your circles of interest are widening."

"Wolf's circles certainly are," Robbie agreed. "At first he merely ran around our garden and buildings. Now he circles the entire farm and your farm, too. He doesn't really need the rabbits he catches."

"Any more than you needed the muskrats you trapped."

"Wolf and I—why do we act the way we do?"

"Instinct! Racial memory! Ingrained habits of the species! Call it what you will. The ancestors of all dogs hunted out of necessity. So did the ancestors of mankind. Survival of the fittest! If you accept Darwin's theory."

"My father does not accept Darwin's theory," Robbie said. "He would probably thrash me if he knew that I had read his *Origin of Species*. He would be very angry with you for lending me the book."

"Of course, Robbie. But he would be unwise if he were to keep you from attending Albion Academy, and later some good college."

"But how will I ever buy my time?"

"That will take a great deal of meditation," the Professor agreed.

During the Christmas vacation when work was slack at the farm, Robbie walked cross-lots to the Henderson ménage with its large barns and stables. Heath Henderson was leaning on the white fence around the oval track where he often exercised and timed his fast trotters.

"Mr. Henderson, you said that if I ever wanted a job . . ."

"Just a minute, Robbie! Watch Charlemagne come down the homestretch. Two minutes and forty seconds. Not bad! Not bad at all. Bubs, you are doing all right."

For the first time Robbie identified the driver of the high-wheeled racing cart, which now turned and came toward them.

Robbie was so astonished and crestfallen and Bubs so disagreeably self-assured that Heath Henderson, who was neither cruel nor insensitive, proved once again that he was a diplomat.

"This isn't the job I meant for you, Robbie. With your head for mental arithmetic, I thought you might start as a junior clerk in Edgerton."

It was Bubs' turn to scowl.

"Thank you kindly," Robbie said, "but I'm still in school. And my paw needs my help. I'd have to buy my time."

"Rub down Charlemagne, Bubs! Be sure to strap on his blanket! Now, Robbie, come with me to the tack room. We have matters to discuss."

That evening at supper, Robbie was obviously bubbling with excitement.

"You were absent quite a bit of the day," his father said coldly.

"I went to Busseyville for the mail," Robbie said, "and then to Heath Henderson's about a job."

"A job?" Ezra exploded. "You've got a job right here."

"And you can't drop out of school," his mother wailed. "I am determined you are going to the Academy."

"Wait a minute, Ellen. I have been very soft-spoken with you. But enough is enough. I am still the head of this household."

Ezra Trent arose, tall and rugged. The lamplight made his shadow on the wall even larger. He was trying to hold his anger within bounds.

"But, Paw. He offered me eight dollars a week."

"Heath must be daft," his father said.

"Oh, Ezra, Ezra, will you never see the light? I have told you, Hannah Hitchcock has told you and Professor Kumlien! Robbie is a very bright boy."

"With eight dollars a week I could . . ." Ezra began.

"You could do nothing," Ellen flared. "If Robbie earns the money it will be his."

It was a disturbed, uncertain and divided family that went to their beds that cold December night.

Robbie loved the wintertime. After harvest, and autumn plowing, there was less farm drudgery. Except for husking and shelling the corn, there were only the morning and evening chores and the splitting and carrying of firewood. If the lakes froze before the first snows came, there were miles of ice for skating. Steel blades rang cheerfully on surfaces which were sometimes as smooth as glass. But if the snows came first, as this year, there was still sledding on the hills; brisk rides in the family cutter; and, most welcome of all, the school bobsled ride on New Year's Eve.

Farmers of the school district took turns in furnishing the team and the bobsled. This year it was Herman Silverwood's turn. His big blacks were shod for snow and ice, as were most of the other horses at this season. To pad his hayrack, he spread a thick layer of clover hay on which at least twenty young people could recline, half buried in hay and covered with buffalo robes.

Miss Hitchcock always presided as chaperone. If any of the smaller children had been given permission by their parents, she sheltered them beside her. She also kept her eye on the eighth graders.

The bobsled was half filled with merry and singing youngsters when Silverwood pulled in at the Trent drive. Robbie and Wolf came running.

"Mr. Silverwood, may I please bring Wolf?"

"If he won't start a runaway."

"He's quite gentle," Hannah Hitchcock assured him. "What do you say, children?"

"Oh, please, Mr. Silverwood!"

Robbie and Wolf leaped into the tangle of gay young people, and Robbie added a buffalo robe to the general cover.

Two stops beyond, they drew up at Inga's house, the sleigh bells tinkling.

"Be very careful, Inga," her mother called from the lamplit doorway.

"We'll take care of her," Hannah Hitchcock promised.

"She'll be safe with Robbie," Celeste Henderson said teasingly.

"Hello, Inga!"

"Hello, Robbie! Everybody!—Behave yourself, Wolf!"

"He's jealous," Celeste said.

After half an hour, clip-clopping along the snowy road, one of the little girls fell asleep with her head in Hannah Hitchcock's lap. Hannah suddenly wished she had a little girl of her own. "But these are all my children!" she told herself quite sharply.

Aloud she said, "Speak softly, please. Susan has gone to sleep."

There was no sound except that of the horses' hooves and the creak of the runners on the granulated snow. The silence of the moonlit night did more than Hannah Hitchcock's gloved finger on her lips to quiet her pupils.

Their conversations were subdued.

"Inga!"

"Yes, Robbie."

"I need your advice."

Inga was startled. Robbie had never before seriously asked her for advice. It made her feel suddenly needed and frighteningly grown up. "If I can help!"

Their voices were little more than whispers.

"Lots of people are poor this year. They've got the wolf at their door. We've got him right inside the cabin."

"But he's an awfully nice wolf," Inga said.

They both petted the shaggy creature who, at the mention of his name, came snuggling up between them.

"You've seen how many of the bigger boys are dropping out of school," Robbie said. "I may have to drop out, too, and maybe take a job."

"But, Robbie, you *mustn't.*"

"So Professor Kumlien says, and Miss Hitchcock, and my mother."

"You can't, Robbie. You *must* go on to the Academy and college. It wouldn't matter if *I* dropped out."

"If I go to the Academy, you'll go with me."

It was the nearest they had ever come to admitting that their lives were in any way intertwined. What Robbie had said hushed them for several thoughtful moments.

"If that is your advice," Robbie said, "I think I will *not* drop out of school. If you and my mother, and Professor Kumlien and Miss Hitchcock all feel the same, you must have a good reason."

More time had passed than they had realized. Herman Silverwood pulled his team to a stop on a hill above the moonlit lake. He held his big stem-winder in the light of the lantern and proclaimed: "Get ready now! One more minute to the New Year."

A few moments later he cried "Happy New Year. Happy eighteen seventy-four!" And all the drowsy children awoke with a great start, shouting the same greeting.

> "Should auld acquaintance be forgot
>   And never brought to mind"

—the voices rang clear over the snowy lake. Once a year it was permitted publicly, and Robbie and Inga now kissed for the first time.

12: The Race Is to the Swift

There hung on the wall of the Trent cabin a ferociously realistic print of a pack of famished wolves pursuing a Russian troika pulled by three terrified horses. In the sleigh an aristocratic man and wife, wrapped in coats of sable, were obviously in a state of panic. As the father leaned forward whipping the horses, the mother glanced back at the wolves. Oddly enough, she seemed to be letting the baby slip over her shoulder. There were many variations on this melodramatic lithograph. Some were entitled "Throwing the Baby to the Wolves."

These prints, which were extremely popular at the time, left little to the imagination. They probably contributed as much to the prejudice against *Canis lupus* as did the story of *Little Red Ridinghood*.

"Would a mother throw her baby to the wolves?"

"Those Russians, they must be absolute monsters!"

"Do wolves actually eat human beings?"

"Couldn't the horses outrun them?"

As a conversation piece, this picture of human sacrifice had few equals. It caused many mid-Victorians to ask themselves guiltily, "Would I doom a child to save my own life?"

When he was a very small boy (and at a time when there were still many wolves howling in the woods of southern Wisconsin), Robbie was both horrified and fascinated by the picture. He talked at an early age. One day he asked his mother:

"Who is that baby?"

"It's *not* you, Robbie."

"Yes it is, and the wolves are going to eat me."

"But you're right here."

"No, I'm not," said the small and stubborn boy. "I'm all eaten up."

Ezra told this over the years as a very funny story. Robbie was always embarrassed. He tried on every possible occasion to show that he was not afraid of Kumlien's dark woods. He was still trying to prove to himself he was not afraid when he crawled into the wolf den to emerge with "the pick of the litter."

Other aspects of the lithograph still intrigued him. He was now reasonably sure that wolves (at least American wolves) do not ordinarily attack and eat human beings. But in a recurring nightmare he found himself driving a very fast horse hitched to the family cutter. Close behind him raced the wolves in the picture. As often as not it was his own gentle wolf-dog whose sympathetic nuzzling awakened the agitated dreamer. Wolf provided his own cure for dreams about wolves.

Thure Kumlien had spent his summer vacations while at Uppsala in extended nature rambles. One summer it was exploration of the Baltic Islands, during which he rediscovered a small roseate gull that had first been seen by Carl Linnaeus, but had been recorded by no other ornithologist in approximately a century.

The next summer had been spent far north in Lapland, where the young naturalist hiked and explored for nearly three months. It was here that he had seen wolves chasing the reindeer (which so closely resemble all the other caribou of the Arctic). During Robbie's questioning, the Professor said, "No, I never saw wolves pull down any caribou in his prime. Sometimes an old or crippled animal, sometimes a sickly calf."

"And how about the relative speed of wolves and deer when there were many of both in this part of Wisconsin?"

"Come to think of it, I never saw the wolves overtake any mature buck or doe. They tried often enough."

"Is that why most herds of grazing animals can survive, even when wolves are among them?"

"You are asking a very good question, Robbie."

"Then you don't believe that picture on our wall?"

"For two excellent reasons," Kumlien said. "I don't believe that even in Russia a mother would throw her baby to the wolves. And I do not believe that three such magnificent horses could be outrun by wolves."

Robbie's nightmare became less frequent, but he would not be satisfied until he tried an experiment. He had told his parents that he was not accepting Henderson's offer of a job. This pleased his father because he could still count upon Robbie's loyal labor in this year when he needed him so badly. It pleased his mother because she was determined that Robbie should continue with his schooling.

"Can I hitch Spinney to the cutter? I promised Mr. Henderson I would let him know."

"Of course," his father said.

"Be careful, Robbie," his mother cautioned.

"I'll be careful," Robbie promised as he and Wolf raced to the stable. "Wolves can certainly run faster than human beings," Robbie admitted to his pet.

Spinney was a lively three-year-old bay mare. Boys in the 1870's knew as much about horses as they would about automobiles a century later. This handsome creature was a Morgan, although she had no papers to prove it. This meant that her breeding went back to Justin Morgan, a remarkably strong, fast little stallion that lived in Vermont in the years when George Washington was the President of the United States. Like her great ancestor, Spinney was exactly fourteen hands (fifty-six inches) high. And like him she was very gentle and willing, able to pull stumps or boulders, plow, cultivate, drag logs out of the woods or step along at a lively clip ahead of a buggy or a sleigh.

Robbie hitched Spinney to the cutter, whistled to Wolf and started the two-mile sleigh ride to Heath Henderson's. He asked no speed of the Morgan, and his wolf-dog had no difficulty in keeping abreast as he ran along the edge of the road. (On the way home Robbie planned to try his experiment.)

But as he turned the corner on the last half mile to Henderson's, he became engaged in a race he had not bargained for. Bubs Mooney, who had been sent on an errand to Fort Atkinson, pulled alongside with Charlemagne attached to a racing sleigh.

"Race you to Henderson's!" Bubs challenged.

"Paw don't want me to race."

It would be far from an even match. Charlemagne, of aristocratic ancestry, stood seventeen hands high. His stride was many feet longer than Spinney's.

Before Robbie knew what Bubs was about, the bully stood up in his sleigh and slashed his whip with all his strength across the rump of the astonished little Morgan, who thereupon shot forward like a ball out of a cannon.

"Tell your paw to shinny on his tintype," Bubs yelled, as he whipped his own horse.

The race was on. The horses knew it, the boys knew it and so did Wolf. Luckily this well-traveled road between Fort Atkinson and Edgerton was wide enough in most places for both sleighs.

For more than three hundred yards, the lightning start of the Morgan kept Robbie well in the lead. But the long, easy stride of Charlemagne began to tell. As they approached a culvert too narrow for both vehicles, Robbie for the first time in his life touched Spinney with his whip, yelling, "Come on, girl!" He pulled toward the center of the road a length ahead of Bubs, who now was whipping Charlemagne furiously. A collision would have meant little to Bubs, tragedy for Robbie. But both boys were now slightly insane with the excitement. A hundred feet behind, Wolf was galloping with all his might, howling like a specter hound.

The heart of the little Morgan was sound and brave. Her legs pumped like pistons. The big shadow to her left seemed to be gaining on her, and the savage sound of the whip sent a tingle along her spine.

"Go it, Spinney!"

"Get going, you son of Satan!"

"Boys! Pull up," Heath Henderson cried. They had crossed the finish line nose and nose.

His first strong words were for Bubs. "If I ever see you whip a horse like that again, you're fired." Then he saw the welt on Spinney's rump. "Which one of you did that?"

Both boys were silent.

"I did," Bubs finally admitted sullenly. "Robbie wouldn't race."

"Well, at least you're truthful," Henderson said, cooling a little from his rage. Henderson was between the two heaving horses, caressing one with each hand.

"I never saw a Morgan travel that fast in my entire life," Henderson said in amazement. "Incredible! And running against Charlemagne. Will you race your little mare next Fourth of July, Robbie?"

"My paw don't want me to race."

"If I give you a racing cart, and a stop watch?"

"Well, I'll ask him! But what is your reason?"

"I like to see a good boy and a good horse have their chance."

That evening at supper Robbie retold the entire story to a rather shocked mother and a strangely gloating father. To beat Heath Henderson at anything would be balm of Gilead to Ezra Trent. He felt he had been cheated all his life by Heath's high prices for farm machinery, and low prices for grain.

"They could put us out of our church," Ezra remembered.

"Not for a *trotting* race," Robbie said.

"That's right," Ezra said. "Not for trotting."

"You might get thrown out of the cart," his mother faltered.

"I can take care of myself, Mom."

"Well, we'll see," Ellen said. "I never thought to bring up a racing driver."

"Know who came in last?" Robbie said happily. "Wolf did."

"What makes you so happy about that?" Ezra wanted to know.

"It means that picture on the wall is a dirty lie."

"Robbie," his mother said, "you are even beginning to talk like a jockey!"

"Careful of your language, son."

"Those wolves couldn't *catch* a fast horse. It's a lie, and I just proved it."

"Then maybe you *weren't* tossed to the wolves," Ezra chuckled.

"I guess that's what I mean," Robbie said, and for no reason at all went over and patted his mother on the cheek.

13: The House-Raising

The verbal invitation had gone out for miles around. The Kumliens were having a house-raising. Margretta and Thure were esteemed neighbors (although thought to be a trifle "queer" in their notions). It was well known, moreover, that Margretta was "not long for this world, poor woman." So out of friendliness, curiosity, sociability and in a few cases morbidity, the farmers and their wives came by surrey, rig and "jolt wagon" on that bright April morning of Margretta's fifty-fourth birthday.

The men brought hammers, mallets, chisels, saws, draw-shaves, axes, adzes and numerous other tools. The women, despite the scarcity of money, vied in their prideful baskets, well laden with cold roast chicken and whole hams, glazed with honey and garnished with cloves. Pickles, preserves, jams, jellies; cakes and pies, loaves of home-baked bread and crocks of home-churned butter; Mason jars of beets, pears, plums; apple butter cooked with cider and flavored with cinnamon—all these seemed to belie and defy the panic.

The men came mostly in overalls, the women in their second-best dresses. Full-length aprons would cover their sober finery when they were preparing the big midday dinner.

Ezra and Ellen Trent were doing their share. Ezra considered himself the best man with adz or broadax in the township. Robbie was always proud to see how his father made the chips fly when he squared a great timber. But

Ezra had a worthy competitor in Big Chris Skavilain, and a contest was expected between them.

As the two contestants carefully surveyed their thirty-six-foot white oak logs, Inga said: "I'm betting on Uncle Chris."

"I'm betting on Paw," Robbie said staunchly.

The "square" was first marked on either end of the log. Then a carpenter's line, heavily chalked, was stretched from one end of the timber to the other. When it was "snapped," the chalk lines showed how the cylindrical length would look when shaped into a square beam.

These foundation timbers to be laid the length of the house were to be joined at the corners by eighteen-foot beams that would then define the first floor of the new dwelling. It was a grand, heart-warming thing to see men as brawny as Ezra and Uncle Chris Skavilain roll up their shirt sleeves and take their broadaxes.

"Hew to the line, let the chips fall where they may."

"Ready! Go!" The pistol shot rang out.

It stirred Ellen to see her big man swing true and sure into the tough white oak, moving down the log and leaving behind him the level surface of the beam. Chris, steady but stolid, also sent great chips flying. He was fifteen years younger than Ezra and breathing easily.

As Ellen watched Ezra, so Inga's mother watched Uncle Chris. Ezra was still ahead at the halfway line, but Big Chris was gaining on him, and the older man was feeling his years.

"Go it, Paw."

"Go it, Uncle Chris."

"Aren't they magnificent?" Margretta Kumlien said as she came carefully from the cabin to rest in her chair on the broad stoop.

"Happy birthday, Margretta; isn't this a lovely day?"

"The loveliest day since the beginning of the world," the older woman said quietly. She saw, as in a vision, her boys and her neighbors putting up her "birthday house."

"How skillfully Ezra wields the broadax."

"He does handle it well," Ellen admitted.

Margretta laughed softly, "Things must be going better at your house."

Ellen felt her cheeks redden. "Yes, Margretta."

"It is always better to make your loved one happy."

"But I lost three babies."

"I also lost my first little girl," Margretta said. "Then came Ludwig, Theodore, Swea Maria and Frithiof."

"How fortunate you are."

"Yes, fortunate, but so ill," Margretta said sadly, yet with vast contentment. "I may not live to move into the new house."

"You mustn't say such a thing."

"But it is true," Margretta said. "I feel like Moses, looking across Jordan into the promised land, but never allowed to enter. See, there will be the parlor, and there the kitchen with the new stove, and our bedroom, Thure's and mine."

"Margretta, you are breaking my heart."

There was a great shout. Big Chris was holding aloft his ax.

Ellen looked, and Ezra still hewed away at his log.

Her heart went out to him.

It is miraculous how rapidly a house can rise with twenty men and a few boys working together. Thure and his three sons had previously dug the cellar, and quarried the limestone for the cellar walls from an outcropping not fifty feet from the house. All clapboards and floor boards and smaller beams were ready and piled.

Thure had told several white lies that made Margretta believe he could afford to build this house which he had promised her for so many years. He exaggerated the amount he was paid for various collections of mounted birds. He told her that the Smithsonian Institution had sent one hundred dollars for his beautifully mounted trumpeter swan when in truth they had paid one-fifth that amount. He said he had been given a salary raise for teaching at Albion Academy. Actually he had silently obtained a loan from Heath Henderson.

Secure in the knowledge of this unbelievable new prosperity, Margretta had been happy in helping Frithiof with his drawings for the new dwelling: here a closet, there a cupboard; here the rare luxury of two hand pumps, one at either end of the kitchen sink; the first pouring forth the pure cold drinking water from the new well; the second providing soft rain water stored in the new cistern.

The four children and Thure kept the secret that this was mostly on money borrowed on a mortgage. They were unable to keep from her the other secret, that she was very ill. Margretta, knowing full well that she was dying, was trying to protect her family from knowledge of the cancer's rapid progress. The children are almost grown, she kept reassuring herself. And their Aunt Sophia will care for them if I should die.

By noon the men were as hungry as bears and the women were eager to feed them. Planks were laid on sawhorses, and the boards covered with white linen and mountains of viands.

Inga felt well attended, with Robbie sitting on her right and fifteen-year-old Frithiof on her left. They chattered happily, and fed Wolf and Ring bites from their plates. When they had finished their meal, Frithiof asked shyly, "Would you like to see some of my paintings, Inga?"

"Of course! Come along, Robbie!"

"Robbie has seen most of them," Frithiof objected.

"I'd like to see them again."

They went up the steep, narrow stairs to the fairly commodious loft, with windows at each end.

"I'll have a real studio in the new house."

"Frithiof! This painting of your mother . . ."

"Do you like it, Inga?"

"I wish you would paint one of me," the girl said. "Then people would remember me, also."

"Remember you?" Frithiof asked, bewildered. "But you are barely thirteen."

Robbie's emotions swirled from acute jealousy to a great sense of impending loss.

"She frequently has a bad dream," he said. "Her mother has frightened her."

"Mother says I will never live to grow up."

Frithiof hesitated, then said, "How would you like it if I painted you in a long dress with your hair in a coil at the nape of your neck?"

"You will paint her in pigtails or not at all," Robbie said, feeling fiercely protective. It was Inga who reacted:

"Robbie, you shall not tell me what to do."

All three were silent for a few unhappy moments. Then Inga in one of her always unpredictable decisions said slowly and firmly, "Thank you, Frithiof. I will put up my hair and borrow one of Mother's long dresses. Taken in a bit, however," she added mischievously.

Robbie did not know whether to laugh or to weep as they all trooped down to join the others in an afternoon of communal labor.

The framing of the house went rapidly. By five o'clock of that sunny afternoon a little green spruce was nailed as the rooftree at the western peak of the dwelling. Now the uprights and crossbeams of the rectangle were in place. Robbie and others had completed the laying and pegging of the white oak first floor. None of the rooms had been partitioned off, so that presently there was a large dance floor under the sky with only a suggestion of roof and outer walls. It was an exciting construction, "like the whitened skeleton of some great animal," Frithiof thought. He began sketching it rapidly on a sheet of drawing paper while Inga watched with fascination.

Hard-working men like to devour three square meals a day. So the women laid out supper before the dance began.

"I have always been against dancing," Ezra said.

"Nonsense, this is only play-party dancing," Ellen implored.

"It is good for the posture," Miss Hitchcock said.

"Just jigs, reels, hornpipes, and quadrilles," Professor Kumlien explained; "all perfectly innocent."

"Well . . . in that case," Ezra said. (How beautiful Ellen was, in her tight-fitting bodice and flaring skirt.)

Several men thought their women were handsome. Big Chris Skavilain looked at his brother's widow and found

her comely. Kathleen O'Neill Skavilain, from the North
of Ireland, had given Inga that sprinkle of freckles across
her nose, and some of her impudence and wit and charm,
but also the young girl's sense of foreboding.

It was a tribute to Wolf that women, who at first had
been frightened by his slanting green eyes and long white
fangs, now patted him as he walked by or pushed him out
of the way as they prepared their youngest for slumber.
Nursing babes were now put in their cradles, or fell
asleep in their mothers' arms. Some trundle-bed young-
'uns, who would rather have kept their eyes wide open,
drowsed among the violets and anemones. Yard children
mostly pumped in the swings under the oak trees. But all
over seven intended to dance. So did a few who were
over seventy, as well as people of all ages in between.
There was little separation of the generations in the days
when everyone worked and played together.

Margretta Kumlien, watching from her vantage point
on the cabin stoop, rocked slowly and serenely. Her beloved Thure and their four living children were all here
and accounted for. Her sister Sophia, who had "chape-
roned" their prenuptial trip to America, was still on hand
to care for the family when Margretta died. And here too
were her friends and neighbors of three decades on the
difficult but beautiful frontier of southern Wisconsin. She
sighed with vast contentment.

Herman Silverwood tuned up his fiddle, Frithiof
strummed preliminary chords on his guitar, and the now
silver-haired Professor piped a few woodland notes upon
his flute. Immediately the whippoorwills began their an-
tiphony—strident, plaintive and haunting.

Herman Silverwood, who also "called the dances," suggested that Robbie and Inga "lead off." But Inga was
suddenly shy and Robbie too unsure of his dance steps.
To everyone's amazement Inga's mother, Kathleen, a vir-
tual recluse since her husband's drowning, moved gracefully to the floor on the arm of Big Chris Skavilain. Others quickly paired off for the Grand March.

Silverwood was a good "caller" and respected the etiquette of the occasion.

"Honor the oldest and the youngest."

This was easy since eighty-three-year-old Barbara Bussey was holding in her arms her first great-great-grandchild, so young that he was still unnamed.

"Bow to the fairest of them all!"

By previous agreement, they bowed to Margretta, whose pale cheeks were suddenly tinged with pleasure. Only the fine bone structure remained of her considerable youthful beauty.

Lusty and gay, almost too gay for the occasion, came the squealing of the fiddle. The chords and glissandi of the guitar were more muted. Frail, wild and lost came the leitmotif of the flute.

"Whippoorwill, whippoorwill," the brown birds insisted.

"Stomp, shuffle, stomp," said the heavy boots of the farmers on the solid new floor.

"Tap, shuffle, tap," answered the lighter feet of the girls and women.

"Allemand right . . . Allemand left."

"You are the 'fairest of them all'!" Robbie said.

Inga swung her pigtails from side to side in silent denial.

When the sun finally disappeared in the west, the full moon came up over Lake Koshkonong's eastern shore. The dancers scarcely needed the lanterns hung from the beams above. Looking up through the airy rafters, they could see a sky filled with stars so large one might have caught them in a butterfly net.

Once during the intricate steps of Portland Fancy, Wolf and Ring chased a big, bushy-tailed raccoon right across the dance floor, knocking one woman flat and causing general hilarity and disarray. The raccoon scrambled up a nearby tree to safety, then screamed at the dogs below. In an agony of frustration, his canine pursuers leaped and howled at the base of the tree until Robbie went over to quiet them.

They had enjoyed "Hull's Victory," "Pop Goes the Weasel," "Money Musk" and many another lively tune. With varying degrees of clumsiness or skill they had gone through the figures of quadrilles, Virginia reels and ga-lops. They had sung and danced to such tunes of the day as "Marching Through Georgia" and "When Johnny Comes Marching Home," which caught at the throats of some whose boys had not returned from the Civil War.

But no music can last forever. It was time to pack bas-kets, gather up children and hitch the drowsy horses.

All came to say good night to their host and hostess. It meant more than a casual farewell to Margretta.

Ellen and Ezra came last, still flushed from their danc-ing.

"Will you help me to bed, Ellen?"

"Do you want me to sit up with you tonight?" Ellen asked as she tucked the comforter around her.

"No, thank you. Thure will be with me."

"It was a lovely house-raising and dance," Ellen said.

"Good night and good-bye, Ellen. Do you remember Shakespeare's *Tempest*? 'We are such stuff as dreams are made on, and our life is rounded with a sleep.'"

"Margretta, you *will* live to enjoy your new house."

"No, Ellen, but I have seen its beautiful beams and rafters." For a long moment she held her neighbor's hand. Then she said, as though remembering it from far away and long ago, "I joined Thure in crossing the Atlan-tic in a leaking ship. We came by way of the canal and the lakes and on into the wilderness. I pitched hay with him, dug potatoes and bore him five children, including that beautiful little girl who died. Good-bye, Ellen."

"Good night, but not good-bye," Ellen said.

Later it seemed to Ellen Trent that her hopeful proph-ecy had been in part fulfilled. Margretta lived for five months beyond that April night, and, for a few of these weeks, in the new house. By the time Ring and Wolf howled the dark news of Margretta's death, Ellen's forth-coming baby was five months along its way.

14: A Boy's Will Is the Wind's Will

One drowsy afternoon not long after the house-raising, Robbie fell asleep at his desk. Miss Hitchcock shook his shoulder gently. "Time for your recitation, Robbie."

"I have no recitation, Miss Hitchcock!"

"Does that remind you of someone?"

"Bubs Mooney, I suppose."

"Exactly! Now, Robbie, I want to speak to you after school."

Inga looked at Robbie in amazement. Never before had he failed to recite. Never had he been compared to the stable boy who lived on the shanty boat. Never, in such a tone of voice, had he been asked to remain after school. Robbie was the brightest boy in miles, and Inga would pull the hair of anyone who said differently. Her recitation was scheduled next. As she arose, she feared she could not control her voice:

"A boy's will is the wind's will,
And the thoughts of youth are long, long thoughts."

She sat down and hid her face in her folded arms.

"What's happening to this seventh-grade class?" Hannah Hitchcock asked her schoolroom. "Bubs drops out, Robbie has no recitation and now Inga's crying."

"And Celeste Henderson is absent," a pert little third grader piped up. "That's the whole seventh grade."

Hannah Hitchcock was not surprised that Bubs had

left school. He was a slow learner and an unhappy student. Celeste was probably on a shopping trip with her mother in Chicago. But Robbie's exhaustion and Inga's moments of brooding were matters of concern.

As she dismissed the school for the day, she was wondering how best to conduct the interview. She decided to begin with a stiff reprimand.

"Robbie Trent, what excuse do you have for your recent lackluster schoolwork?"

Robbie said nothing. Inga was lingering at her desk, and Robbie did not want her to hear what he was about to tell Miss Hitchcock.

"Fasten your book strap and be on your way, Inga."

"Yes, Miss Hitchcock."

"Now, Robbie, I want to hear all about it."

"Well it begins each year with stripping the tobacco, then lambing time, and then the endless spring plowing. Always there are dreary chores, night and morning."

"But you carried all this work last year, and the year before."

"We usually had a hired man to help us."

"There is something more that you are not telling me, Robbie."

Robbie was silent for a moment. He looked out at the clear afternoon sunlight which fell like a slanting shower of luminous green rain through the new leaves. As he watched, a cloud began drifting across the sun. In another moment all the luminosity had faded. Killdeers were crying.

"I've got to win that race."

"What race?"

"The one on Fourth of July. The trotting race."

"I didn't even know that you owned a race horse," his teacher said.

"We don't. We just have Spinney. But I've got to win."

"Robbie Trent. Will you go back to the very beginning and let me know what you are talking about!"

Robbie sighed wearily. "It started years ago when I was smaller. In those days Bubs Mooney was much bigger and stronger than I. Every time I met him he threatened to cut my ears off. He still bullies fourth and fifth graders."

"Why didn't you tell your father?"

"Miss Hitchcock, no boy can tell his father. Paw would have laughed at me. A boy has to fight his own battles in this world."

"I'm glad I used my ruler on that rapscallion."

"Your ruler didn't help either. Nor his paw's thrashings. He just took it out on smaller boys. And then last summer, when Wolf was a mere puppy, he started sicking his big mean white dog on my good little wolfling."

"Wolf will take care of himself one of these days."

"I hope so," Robbie said, "but Bubs is *my* problem. Do you know he stole all my traps last autumn?"

"Your mother told me."

"And now that he's working for Heath Henderson and driving Charlemagne, he thinks he's the king of the road."

"So you're training Spinney to race Charlemagne?"

The sky had grown even dimmer. A few large drops splattered on the schoolhouse roof. Thunder rumbled like a wheel across some distant bridge. The world was breathless, waiting for the downpour.

"I'm not racing against Charlemagne. I'm racing against Bubs."

"I think I'm beginning to understand," Miss Hitchcock said.

"Late every evening, after the chores, Paw lets me hitch the racing cart to Spinney."

"When you are both bone weary," his teacher added compassionately.

"I don't have much time to read my lessons, Miss Hitchcock."

The rain was now pelting down, bringing the fragrance of ozone and wet grass. Robbie helped his teacher close the windows. Then he strapped together his books and slate.

"That boy isn't worth your worry, Robbie," Miss Hitchcock protested loudly over the rush of the rain. "What does it matter if you win or lose a mere horse race? You are thoughtful and decent. You'll go on to the Academy and college and have a brilliant career. You've taken a wrong turn, Robbie. But it isn't too late to change your course."

"Thank you, Miss Hitchcock. But first I have to win that race."

The shower stopped as suddenly as it began.

Robbie stepped from the door marked BOYS into a rain-washed world. Then he saw Inga outside the door marked GIRLS. She was drenched, and even the books she had shielded from the rain were damp.

"I waited for you, Robbie. I had to."

"You're soaking wet."

"That doesn't matter."

They walked down the path together. He put his dry jacket over her slender shoulders.

"What did you tell Miss Hitchcock?"

So Robbie repeated his story. And for his pains he was given a second scolding, and more of the same advice.

"Who cares whether you win over Bubs?"

"I do."

"He's just a miserable river rat."

"He's human," Robbie said, to his own surprise. "And he's my mortal enemy."

"Oh, Robbie, you're so stubborn."

"So are you, Inga."

For some reason this seemed to them deeply and tenderly amusing. They walked beside each other in silence to the place where each afternoon they had to part.

"Good-bye, you stubborn boy."

"Good-bye, you stubborn, pretty girl."

Robbie came upon Thure Kumlien drawing water at his spring. The Professor's face was tired but uplifted in the rain-washed, late-afternoon sunshine.

"How is Mrs. Kumlien?"

"She is still with us."

"Will you finish the house in time?"

"Barely, I think. But, Robbie, you too look tired. What is troubling you?"

And so for the third time that day Robbie explained his dilemma.

"If I am not the strongest nor the swiftest . . . ?" Robbie asked.

"You may still be the wisest."

"I am even doing poorly in my schoolwork."

"Forget the horse race, Robbie. Get back to your books. Someday you may be a famous scholar."

"After I win the race with Bubs," Robbie insisted.

"Aren't you thinking too much about yourself?"

"Perhaps."

"Robbie, you are a very intelligent boy. But, like the rest of us, you still have a great deal to learn."

"Somehow I must find time next Saturday to help you put the shingles on your roof," Robbie said.

Robbie was afraid that his father would scold him for being kept after school. He thought that he would be reprimanded for coming home too late to help with the chores. But to his surprise all that his father said was, "You and Spinney should both be well rested. Neither of you has done a lick of work all day."

"So you still want me to win that race on the Fourth of July?"

"Son, that's the most important race we will ever run. Our Spinney will beat Heath Henderson's Charlemagne. If I wasn't a deacon of the church, I'd bet on it."

After supper, Robbie, whose day had been as wearing as though he had worked in the field, hitched the little Morgan to the racing cart. The seat was wide enough to carry double—one boy and one wolf-dog. Spinney had outrun Wolf so often that Robbie felt sorry for his sensitive pet. He had fastened, as a toehold, a strip of two-inch lumber on Wolf's side of the seat. It gave his forepaws sufficient support so that he could become an avid co-driver.

Robbie whistled between his fingers. Wolf came dashing to make a flying leap into his place. Spinney felt equally eager for the evening run.

Many of the local roads ran squarely around a section,

one mile north, east, south and west. Since the Ordinance of 1787, the Middle West had been laid out square with the world, giving many Midwesterners then and since a sense of direction, and a solid image of their country.

"Tonight we're going to make a record," Robbie said to Wolf and Spinney.

When they reached the corner, Robbie pressed the stem of his stop watch while slapping the reins across Spinney's back.

"Go it, girl! Get going, Spinney!"

Boy and wolf-dog leaned forward for the swift whirl down this particular mile. The rail fence rippled backward as the cart devoured the yardage.

"Faster, Spinney, faster!"

The Morgan responded marvelously to Robbie's voice. Her sure little feet drove the earth behind her.

"Faster, Spinney. You're making it, girl!"

As they reached the next corner, Robbie snapped the watch.

"Two minutes and forty seconds! First time we ever did it."

The excited horse whinnied. Wolf howled, musically. Then Robbie and Wolf leaped out of the cart to cavort around the great little Morgan.

"They can keep their good advice. We're going to win that race on the Fourth of July."

15: Preparation for the Big Event

Heath Henderson's gift of the lightweight cart had sharpened Robbie's eyes to other examples of the wainwright's artistry. Carriage makers of the nineteenth century were as dextrous in their designs as automobile makers one hundred years later. The beautiful ways in which they curved, paneled, varnished and decorated these streamlined conveyances emphasized the importance of speed. But they also emphasized the importance of courtship. The racing sleighs, and even some of the racing carts, had room for one passenger beside the driver. When not actually racing, the driver and his partner were part of the passing parade.

Currier and Ives and other lithographers paid minute attention to horses. On the walls of Henderson's tack room were portraits, real or imaginary, of some of the fabled horses of the past. Here, for example, was Messenger, the gray thoroughbred imported from England in 1788, whose royal blood coursed through the arteries of some of the fastest horses in America. Here too was his famous grandson, Topgallant, who had trotted the first recorded three-minute mile. Seconds had been clipped from that three minutes in almost every great race since.

"Charlemagne is a blue blood."

"You don't think Spinney and I have a chance?"

"Frankly, no!" Henderson said. "But may the best boy and the best horse win!"

Robbie had one advantage. He was an avid reader, quick to learn. He borrowed from the bookcase in the tack room *English Racer and Saddle Horse* by Thomas Hookham, as well as several other volumes and pamphlets on the care and training of horses. Bubs, who read slowly and painfully, was scornful.

"You can't learn about horses from books."

"No, but it helps," Robbie said.

And indeed Robbie did learn faster, and retain more of the information, when Henderson showed them how to balance a horse's diet, how to mix and apply liniment, and how to bandage, neatly and firmly, a weak or sprained joint.

Robbie drove more carefully, less arrogantly, than Bubs. And he retained the affection of the horse he drove.

Bubs never again lashed Charlemagne during this training period, at least not within view of the owner. But Henderson had reason to suspect that a feud was developing between the trotter and his young driver.

In the pre-panic days, Henderson had employed a trainer, a racing driver and a stableboy, and had kept a dozen horses. Now he felt he must "play poor." With six horses, and only one novice for all duties, he was telling his neighbors that even a prosperous merchant must cut corners in such a deep and long depression.

Henderson retained Bubs for additional reasons. Young Mooney had a fighting will to win. Carefully directed, he might become a good racing driver. Heath had long since proved to himself that a cantankerous horse can be gentled. Possibly so might a boy. He had a long talk with Bubs and raised him from three dollars to four dollars a week.

"But you two young men must work hard during the next few weeks."

"I ain't quite sure who you're betting on," Bubs said with distrust.

Henderson chuckled. "That's a good question, Bubs. I'm not quite sure myself."

At supper that evening Robbie did not plead for himself, but he did plead for Spinney. "Paw, you can't slave that little Morgan all day and expect her to win the race."

"That also goes for Robbie," Ellen said.

"The boy will be all right," Ezra contended. "But to rest Spinney, we might use the mule tomorrow."

So, on the following morning, Robbie hitched the stubborn mule to the single cultivator and started through the corn, already knee-high ten days before the Fourth of July.

Ellen must have told Ezra something very heartening. As Robbie came in for noon dinner, his father said, "Robbie, how would you and Spinney like a whole free day? You might take Inga for a drive."

"And a picnic lunch," his mother added. "I'll furnish dessert."

"That would be wonderful," Robbie said, "but what are we celebrating?"

"Your mother says you are going to have a little brother."

"Or sister," Ellen said happily.

"Well, gee whiz, that's certainly something to celebrate," Robbie said. He didn't start feeling the first faint pangs of jealousy for several hours.

On the way over to Skavilain's Point, Wolf sat beside Robbie in his accustomed place. Inga came from the house, swinging a picnic basket in one hand and the chin strap of her straw hat in the other. She wore blue calico and was whistling "Nellie Wildwood."

"Get out of my place, you dog in the manger."

Wolf licked her cheek. She didn't sound very dangerous to him.

Robbie shoved his pet, unceremoniously, to the drive below.

"This seat may be uncomfortable, Inga."

"I know what we need," Inga said. "A fat sofa pillow." She ran back to the house, and returned in a minute

with a green plush pillow on which was embroidered a big red heart with an arrow through it.

"Did you embroider that thing just for our picnic?" Robbie asked.

"Mother embroidered it for Uncle Chris."

"Wonders will never cease," Robbie said.

Inga put the pillow on Wolf's side. It gave her a comfortably upholstered seat.

"Won't your mother be mad? I mean using her fancy pillow?"

"My mother's not mad about anything any more. Where are we going, Robbie?"

"To the hill where we stopped on New Year's Eve."

"Tell Spinney we want to go fast."

"Hang on, Inga."

And off they went in a beautifully varnished cart behind a fast little Morgan who tossed her head in sheer delight and made her mane fly like a silken shawl in the lake breeze.

"She's a fast horse, Robbie."

"We're going to win that race."

"And then what?"

"I'm going to race her at county fairs."

Inga was silent.

"Well, say something! Don't you want me to win, Inga?"

"I don't want to spoil this beautiful day. Please drive slower, Robbie. We're coming to Lotus Lake and I want to see those big yellow water lilies and that beautiful swan."

The boy gently pulled the reins. Spinney had a sensitive mouth. She slowed her pace to a walk.

"What is the Latin name for these flowers?"

"*Nel . . . Nelumbo* something," Robbie faltered. He pulled Spinney to a stop.

"You knew it last year."

"*Nelumbo lutea,*" the boy said triumphantly.

"Oh, Robbie," Inga sighed, "will there be time in your fast new world for swans and lotus blossoms and wolflings?"

Wolf, who by this time had caught up, acted as though he understood Inga's question. He looked up pleadingly.

"You really don't want me to win, do you, Inga?"

"Not if it means changing your whole life."

"But how will I ever buy my time? I thought, with a few purses . . ."

"How much is the prize on the Fourth of July?"

"One hundred dollars to win, fifty to place, twenty-five to show."

The trumpeter swan, with neck beautifully arched, kept the other water birds from his mate's hidden nest.

"That's a late nesting," Robbie said in the ensuing silence.

"You are even talking a new language: 'win, place and show'!"

Robbie clucked to the bay mare, who again began to trot. The well-greased wheels spun noiselessly through the dust. The boy and girl were silent for several minutes as they climbed the hill where, on the moment of midnight, they had welcomed the new year.

In the small grove of great oak trees that crowned this hill, a driven artesian well flowed from a two-inch pipe into a tank that all might use, a stream of water so fresh and cold that it could have been a fountain in the Garden of Eden. Robbie leaped out and offered his help to Inga, who tossed herself into his outstretched arms. (No one fears sprains or broken bones going-on fourteen.)

As Inga spread their ample lunch on the cloth, Wolf added to his sensual knowledge, news of each trespass of chipmunk, rabbit, woodchuck or squirrel. From this vantage point all three could view every mile of their world, mostly a friendly world of farms and villages. Eastward lay Busseyville with its two mills. There was water enough this summer so that both water wheels could be used simultaneously. On this clear day they could see the little wheels turning slowly, sunlight flashing from the falling water.

Westward lay Albion with its three brick Academy buildings on the tree-lined village square.

"I have so much news to tell you, Inga."

"And I to you."

"Mom is going to . . ." Robbie stopped in embarrassment.

"Have a baby? How exciting. Are you going to be jealous?"

"Maybe at first, a little."

"I know I'm going to be jealous," Inga said.

"Jealous of what?"

"When Mother marries Uncle Chris, and they have a baby."

"Things are certainly happening around here," Robbie said.

"They certainly are. The wedding is being held on the Fourth of July, about sixty miles from here at Pine Lake."

"Then you won't see the race?" Robbie said sadly.

"I might," Inga said. "I'm considering."

So much was happening so rapidly that Robbie's head was in a whirl. Evidently Big Chris, the brother of Inga's dead father, was taking Inga's mother back to the first Swedish settlement in Wisconsin to get married.

"That's where the Swedish Lutheran minister lives," Inga explained. "Then Mother and Chris will take a two-week honeymoon on a Lake Michigan steamer. So I could, if I wish, stay home and see the race, but I'm not promising."

While they ate their long, leisurely lunch on the grass, Spinney grazed and Wolf roamed. Now and then the fierce-looking wolf-dog came playfully to the edge of the cloth to beg a piece of cold chicken. The south wind sprinkled whitecaps across the wide blue expanse of Lake Koshkonong.

"Suppose you lost, Robbie!"

"If I lost, I would never be able to buy my time. I would work without pay until I came of age. I would probably never leave the farm, never go to the Academy and college."

"How much does your father want?"

"Three hundred dollars," Robbie said in despair. "And Albion Academy will cost me nine additional dollars a term."

"But to be free, to be utterly free forever?"

"I think that's what Paw means."

"You'd better get a paper in writing, Robbie."

"What's the use? Unless Spinney and I win race after race!"

"There is another way, Robbie. I've been thinking very hard about it."

The boy looked with wonder into the earnest face of the pretty Swedish-Irish girl. It was as though he had never really seen her before. She was still thirteen, still had a sprinkle of freckles across her nose, and eyes as blue as the lake below them. But never before had he really noticed the firmness of her cheekbones and chin, delicate but determined.

"By what miracle . . . ?" Robbie began. He was not quite certain what miracle he was talking about.

"By the miracle of good thinking and hard work."

"Inga, you amaze me."

"First we will rent two acres of good land."

"That would cost at least five dollars a year."

"And then we will plant it to tobacco."

"But, Inga, you have no idea of the labor."

"I have worked in tobacco, just as you have."

"You mean you would help me?"

"We would work together in the summer, Robbie, setting out the plants, hoeing, cultivating, harvesting. Everything!"

"You would do that for me?"

"While I live."

The proposal was almost too overwhelming for Robbie to bear. He took his clean bandanna handkerchief from his pocket and wiped her tears and his own.

"But first you must skip eighth grade. I have already asked Miss Hitchcock if she will give you the tests. She will, and you will pass them with colors flying."

"Wait a minute, Inga."

"Are you angry, Robbie?"

"Not angry, exactly. But aren't you planning my future as though, as though . . . ?"

"As though I were your wife! Well, somebody has to show a little sense around here."

After lunch they gathered up Inga's basket, hitched Spinney to the cart and called Wolf. By common consent they drove by way of Albion to look at the Academy.

"Are you staying home to see me race?"

"If you'll take the eighth grade exams."

"But first I'll win the race."

"Or lose it," Inga said.

"Just as stubborn as ever," Robbie said. They were now on a lonely stretch of road. So, for the second time in their young lives, they kissed.

16: The Fourth of July

On the third of July, Big Chris and Inga's mother started eastward for their Pine Lake wedding.

Grandpa and Inga were trusted to take good care of each other until the honeymooners returned. On the morning of the fourth, Grandpa asked Inga, "Do you want to ride with me in the buggy, or with Robbie in his crazy race cart?"

"If you don't mind, Grandpa . . ."

"I thought as much. Speed, speed, speed, that's all you young folks think about."

"You're wrong there," Inga said. "I hope he loses his race."

"You do?" Grandpa asked in astonishment. They cleared and washed the breakfast dishes together. "Women have always been a mystery to me," the old man confided. "Your grandma could lead me around with her little finger. Your mother has been a real worry ever since she was widowed. And now you want Robbie to lose his race."

"I'm not being stupid, Grandpa."

"I'm sure you're not, Inga. But you *are* unpredictable. Now run along and get ready," the gentle old Viking said. "Robbie will be here any minute."

Throughout the nineteenth century the Fourth of July was at least as important as Christmas in the lives of young Americans. Even though few knew the entire Declaration of Independence by heart, many knew the opening lines. A scattering of the orators of that time really were "silver-tongued." And when their words rolled out mellifluously, and the American flag snapped in the breeze, an earlier, simpler generation knew without question that they loved their country.

The philosophy of the Declaration still guided the beliefs of the more thoughtful citizens.

"We hold these truths to be self-evident, that all men are created equal, that they are endowed by their Creator with certain inalienable Rights, that among these are Life, Liberty and the pursuit of Happiness. . . ."

It must be admitted that most of the children who awoke before dawn to blow off thousands of firecrackers were more interested in the cascade of noise than in American history. But, from the first predawn explosion to the last of the rockets bursting against the midnight sky, the Fourth was largely joyous.

As Spinney pulled the cart to the crest of Long's Hill, the town of Edgerton lay in holiday garb below them. On its northern edge blossomed the Irish Picnic Grounds with its one-mile oval, several tents, many booths and rows of bleachers. From the hilltop all this was seen in miniature—ladies with bright parasols, roustabouts erecting the big top, horses with red, white and blue plumes fastened to their bridles, flags and pennants blowing, the circus ringmaster in a high silk hat and scarlet coat on a shining black charger, about to start the parade.

"We must get there immediately," Inga said.

"But not so fast as to tire Spinney," Robbie reminded her.

Taking a short cut, they were able to avoid the crowded town, and within fifteen minutes had purchased their tickets at the bunting-draped entrance gate. Wolf, who had trotted peacefully beside them, was now snapped to a leash. Spinney was taken to a box stall in the racing stable, and Inga and Robbie were free to find seats in the bleachers while the parade curved by.

The mile of race track barely accommodated the Civil

War veterans in blue with their drum and bugle corps, the troupe of the small circus which included three clowns, one lion and one elephant, the Masons, the Knights of Columbus, and a mob of disorganized boys and girls trying to find their marching units.

"Well, that saves us twenty-five cents apiece," Inga said.

"How so?" Robbie asked.

"We've seen the elephant and we don't need to go to the circus."

After the parade, Inga and Robbie stood for a time listening to a particularly eloquent barker outside a large tent that housed THE CIVIL WAR CYCLORAMA.

"You'll never forgive yourself if you miss the Civil War," the thin veteran said. "Every rousing moment from the Firing on Fort Sumter to the Surrender at Appomattox."

Partly because one sleeve of his uniform was empty and neatly pinned at the cuff, and partly because the voice was brave but haunted, they stood and listened.

"Yes, I was there myself. Lost my arm at Shiloh. But I would do it again, God willing.

"See the carriages of the Senators fleeing back to Washington during the First Battle of Bull Run. Thought it was a picnic, they did, until Stonewall Jackson gave them a whiff or two of grapeshot. War is no picnic, folks. But you won't be shot watching this moving cyclorama.

"See the *Monitor* fighting the *Merrimac*. *Monitor* looks like a cheesebox on a raft. Five solid hours they fought.

"See the gunboats shelling Vicksburg, see Pickett's charge at Gettysburg, and watch the boys in gray mowed down. Don't duck when you hear the sound of shot and shell. Nothing but yards and yards of painted canvas, turned by an old horse on a treadmill out behind the tent.

"Guns that can no longer kill. Drums that no longer beat. Wounds that no longer bleed. And for what purpose, you may ask. So that our black brethren may be 'thenceforward and forever FREE.'

"Here they all are: the generals, great and small—

McDowell, McClellan, Burnside, Hooker and Meade. And Ulysses S. Grant smoking his big cigar! Who will ever forget his ferocious engagements in the Wilderness, at Spotsylvania Court House, Cold Harbor and Petersburg?

"But the general is still alive. Many of the boys are dead who made him famous.

"Right this way, folks; twenty-five cents to see the Civil War in twenty-five minutes! One thin quarter for the whole shebang. All the Civil War you will ever want to experience."

"We should see it," Robbie said doubtfully.

"Not today," Inga said. "It's too sad."

Wolf had always been gentle with small children. So toddlers, who had never been taught fear, sought to pet his head or grasp his fur. One glance of the mother usually produced a terrified scream as she yanked her child to safety.

"He won't bite," Robbie said.

"He's a good Wolf," Inga added.

As boy, girl and Wolf walked along the midway, they happened to meet the ringmaster. "What have you there? As I live and breathe, a genuine, full-blooded, ferocious American timber wolf."

"Part wolf," Robbie corrected. "And never ferocious."

"We would fix that in a hurry," said the tall man in the red coat. "Can he howl?"

"Howl for the ringmaster," Robbie commanded. "Awa —ooh—."

Wolf lifted his great muzzle and howled with such conviction that startled citizens were frozen in their tracks.

One imbiber rubbed his hand slowly across his face and looked again, "Never touch another drop in me life, so help me St. Patrick!"

"Young man, you have a fascinating attraction in that animal. Would you sell him to me for ten dollars?"

"I wouldn't sell him for ten thousand dollars," Robbie said.

"You'd put him in a cage," Inga said indignantly.

"Well, if you ever change your mind . . ."

Eyes followed this trio as they entered the display and registration tent of the Grange. Inside were samples of seed corn and other grains as well as agricultural equipment and machinery. Banners and posters fairly shouted: DOWN WITH THE STOCKYARDS RING, FAIR FREIGHT RATES FOR THE FARMER.

Robbie and Inga would never have dreamed that they might find Heath Henderson in such a center of rural protest.

"Hello, Inga! Robbie!"

"Hello, Mr. Henderson!"

"I see by your startled look that you wonder why I am here."

"I am curious," Robbie admitted.

"Always watch the opposition, young man. Keep track of your competitors. Now, look at this grain reaper."

"It's very much like the McCormick you sold Paw for two hundred and seventy-five dollars."

"And this one, built by a cooperative concern owned by the Grange, has a price tag of one hundred and seventy-five dollars."

"How do you explain that?" Robbie asked with a trace of anger.

"The McCormick people are not in business for charity," Henderson said quietly, "and neither am I. But now we'll have to find some way to cut our margins."

"You don't sound either frightened or furious," Robbie said.

"On the whole the Grange is a good thing," Henderson said. "It's big enough to counter the railroad lobby. That helps all of us as freight rates go down. And competition is always healthy—like a horse race, for instance."

"I'm going to win that race," Robbie said with a touch of defiance.

"That's the spirit, Robbie."

"But I still can't understand your motive," Robbie said. "This Amateur Sweepstakes of yours must cost you a lot of money. You are paying the ten dollars entrance fee for each of the eight of us who are racing. You put up the purse—first, second and third, so that even if your horse wins . . ."

"I still lose," Henderson chuckled.

"I think I understand," Inga said. "You're testing boys, not horses."

Heath Henderson looked at her with astonishment. "How could you possibly have arrived at that conclusion?"

"Because I'm pulling for Robbie to lose so that he can win."

"She means that if I lose the race, I'll probably quit racing and go back seriously to my studies."

"Miss Hitchcock is going to let Robbie take his eighth grade exams so he can skip a year and go right into Albion Academy after seventh grade."

"You are the most complicated but clearheaded youngsters," Heath Henderson said in charmed bewilderment.

Inga had one more surprise for Robbie that morning. She led him to a modest tent at the end of the midway where several local artists had hung their pictures.

Directly facing the door on the back wall of the tent was a three-quarters-life-size portrait of Inga which was by far the best thing Frithiof Kumlien had ever done. Her hair was beautifully but simply arranged at the nape of her neck, and the long gown of her mother, "taken in a little," only emphasized the first moments of young maturity. Frithiof had no right to know so much about Inga. Robbie was both jealous and fiercely proud.

"What do you think?"

"You should *first* have put up your hair for me."

"About the painting, silly?"

"I would give everything I have in the world for it."

"Frithiof gave it to me, and I am giving it to you . . . if . . . !"

"You mean if I lose?" Robbie asked in anguish.

"Win or lose," she said, having let him suffer for just a moment. "It will be your Christmas present."

Heath Henderson's Amateur Sweepstakes was the only horse race run at the oval at the Irish Picnic Grounds on the Fourth of July. More professional racing could be enjoyed on other occasions. But on this particular day the concentration was on the younger citizens, who competed in three-legged races, potato-sack races, pie-eating contests, track events and the baseball game.

The Amateur Sweepstakes, however, was the high point of the afternoon. As Inga had surmised, Henderson was testing boys rather than horses.

"The only really great race is the Human Race," Heath once said at a GAR banquet. And his remark was greeted with such applause he was tempted to repeat himself. Nevertheless he sincerely believed that the best way to judge a boy's character was by watching him drive in a horse race.

It was almost impossible to be disqualified for this race. Any boy with any horse could enter. The judges, all of them friends of Henderson, viewed with great tolerance the inept young drivers and the fractious horses.

As the hour approached, Robbie and the other drivers donned the colored caps and shirts provided by Henderson. These "silks" seldom represented a stable. They merely made it possible to distinguish the drivers, particularly on the backstretch, which was far from the grandstand.

Robbie's garb was crimson. Bubs wore huntsman green. The six others had an assortment of vivid colors. Most of the horses were beautifully groomed, and the afternoon was clear and relatively cool.

Near the starting line sat Robbie's mother and father, Inga, Grandpa Skavilain and Miss Hitchcock. Inga had been instructed to hold tightly to Wolf's leash.

"Not that I wouldn't like him on the seat beside me," Robbie said.

"Be careful of yourself," Inga pleaded.

Only one horse had been scratched.

The seven remaining boys drew for their positions. A

gangling lad driving a huge gray gelding won the coveted rail position. Robbie was second. Four teen-agers from as many neighboring towns ranged outward in the third, fourth, fifth and sixth positions. Bubs Mooney, driving the only thoroughbred on the track, was number seven and obviously enraged by his bad luck.

Horses can sense the mood of their drivers. Fear breeds fear. Confidence breeds confidence. Robbie and Spinney, who were the best of friends, moved up to the starting line with the discipline of veterans. Meanwhile most of the other boys were having trouble. The feud between Bubs and Charlemagne had become so intense that the roan stallion now became all but unmanageable. He bit at the horse to his left as Bubs yanked his entry into line. Charlemagne reared and whinnied. Heath Henderson, who thought of Bubs as a "hard-luck kid," had reason once again to question his choice of driver.

When at last the horses were aligned, Robbie looked back and waved at Inga, who was doing her best to keep Wolf off the track. How did she instantly understand his unspoken message? At that very moment, with the gong about to be sounded, she unsnapped Wolf, who dashed the thirty-five intervening feet and made a single clean leap into his place beside Robbie. Meanwhile a prankster tossed a fuse-lit cannon cracker.

Too late now to stop the stroke of the gong, or the simultaneous blast of the cracker! Spinney leaped forward as from a catapult. The big gray gelding proved his inexperience by breaking into a full gallop. Far out in seventh position Charlemagne reared again before Bubs, with a lash and a curse, started him wheeling down the track.

"Hey, this is a trotting race," Robbie yelled at the gangling boy.

"Tell that to my horse," the boy yelled back. However, he tried to slow the gray to a trot, which cost him several yards.

This was Robbie's chance to gain the rail, a position he never lost to the end of the race. Wolf proved extremely helpful. At first, he was neither barking nor howling, but his very presence swerved other horses and drivers wide of Robbie's cart.

At the quarter post Robbie was two lengths ahead of the gray, and three lengths ahead of the slow-starting Charlemagne, who was still on the far outside of the track. On this first turn, as the carts began to bunch, Wolf barked a sharp warning.

The horses understood. It was anyone's race down the backstretch, as the longer strides of the big gray and of Charlemagne began to tell.

"Come on, Spinney!" Robbie urged.

At the far end of the oval, Bubs started making his bid. Nearly abreast of Spinney, the boy from the shanty boat began beating his thoroughbred with such savagery that the roan put forth every effort to get away from the devil behind him.

The crowd from the very first had gone wild with excitement and laughter.

"Is that a dog?"

"No, by Jupiter, it's a wolf."

"Go it, boy, go it, wolf!"

Not even Heath Henderson was pulling for his brutal young driver.

There at the far end of the oval, Bubs cut in mercilessly, crowding the other horses. He intended to win this race if he had to kill the whole pack. Meanwhile Wolf went into a Wagnerian chorus of barks and howls, frightening these same horses outward.

Smash! The four-horse wreck put all but Spinney, Charlemagne and the gray out of the running. There were shouts of anger from the drivers, wild whinnies from the horses. But what was sheer terror to the participants was a Roman holiday to the mob in the grandstand. They roared with glee.

"Shut up, Wolf!" Robbie shouted. And for a moment his startled pet obeyed.

However, when Bubs tried to come around them to the rail, Wolf growled so fiercely that Charlemagne shied outward. This had been a day infested with devils for the poor thoroughbred, who was still being slashed unmercifully by his crazed driver.

Ears back, necks stretched forward, Spinney and Charlemagne came down the homestretch, with Wolf now howling the fierce howl of expected victory.

Far back at the three-quarters post the other horses and young drivers were sorting themselves out, amazingly undamaged except for one racing cart. They got under way again just as Charlemagne reached the wire, victor by a nose over the greathearted little Morgan.

The winner stood with only a few admirers, as the crowd gathered around Robbie, Spinney and Wolf.

Heath Henderson quieted the spectators to award the prizes. "To coin a phrase," he said, "it matters not who wins. It's the way one wins that matters."

Bubs was given his first, Robbie his second and the gangling lad his third. The money was in the gold coins of the realm, still legal tender in that time of simpler values.

"Three cheers for Robbie, Spinney and Wolf!"

The response was deafening.

"We old folks had better be starting homeward," Grandpa Skavilain said.

Ellen nudged Ezra. "Oh, of course," he said belatedly. "You mean to relieve the young folks of the evening chores?"

"That was the general idea," Ellen said.

The nocturnal fireworks, handled by an able pyrotechnician, sent rocket after rocket soaring to burst against the black velvet bowl of night.

At last Robbie and Inga harnessed Spinney to the cart and by starlight began the leisurely return journey to their homes. Wolf and Spinney could see very well in the dark.

"I'm going to study hard during the month of August," Robbie said.

"I was hoping you would say that."

"Somehow my lifelong contest with Bubs seems only a nightmare."

"We are both losing our nightmares," Inga said.

"I think I have driven my last race," Robbie said a little sadly.

"But Spinney will be the smartest, fastest little Morgan on the road. She'll be taking us both to the Academy next autumn."

"*Both* of us?"

"I have already taken my eighth grade examinations," Inga said. "But your marks will be even higher."

"We still have many problems," Robbie said. "We'll both have plenty of work on our hands."

"Who's afraid of hard work?"

"Or extra study with Kumlien for our teacher!"

They sat for a few moments at Inga's gate. Wolf circled them in a magic ring. The cicadas were shrilling. One whippoorwill spoke to another. Grandpa Skavilain came with his lantern held high. His voice had the faintest hint of a quaver.

"Are you all right, Inga?"

"I've never been all righter."

AUTHOR'S POSTSCRIPT

As the title of this book indicates, I have told the story of Wolf from his birth to his late adolescence. Someday I may write the wilder story of his maturity, and how by fortuitous circumstance he was taken to the unbroken wilderness far to the north.

Wolves may be partly "tamed" to become pets. But I do not recommend the experiment. It is far easier to reverse the process. Deep in their hearts there lingers the strong lupine urge to be utterly free and unfettered. Released from human bondage, they roam the forests, and in their second or third year take a lifelong mate with whom to raise shaggy and beloved offspring.

The leader of such a pack must have great endurance and courage. He must take the major responsibility for his entire "family," which may consist of a grandmother or grandfather and several aunts and uncles besides the mated pair and their pups. Ousted for a few days, the proud father guards the den from some nearby knoll and brings food aplenty to the entrance of the lair to feed the whelping mother and the wolflings.

A very few wolves still survive south of the Canadian border in northern Wisconsin, Michigan, and Minnesota. If you are in that region and have extraordinarily good luck, you may still hear, some moonlit night, the wild, spine-chilling howl of a remote descendant of Wolf himself, "Awa—oooh—ooh, awa ooooooooo!"

Documentary Notes

One Hundred Years Ago

page 1 My father, David Willard North, was born August 10, 1862, in a log cabin on the line between Jefferson and Dane County in southern Wisconsin. He died on January 7, 1962. He was educated at nearby Albion Academy, at Lawrence College in Appleton, Wisconsin, and at the University of Wisconsin.

Letters which he wrote to me when he was eighty years of age furnish some of the background material for this book.

Although he is not the *exclusive* prototype of Robbie Trent, he did have some of Robbie's characteristics.

page 1 Just over the zigzag rail fence lived the Swedish-American naturalist Thure Ludwig Theodore Kumlien (1819-1888). He was born at Hertrop in Härlunda parish in Sweden, and was graduated from Uppsala University with highest honors. While at the university he met Margretta Christine Wallberg, whom he described as "the most beautiful girl of all this nation of handsome women." With her older sister Sophia Wallberg for a companion, the affianced couple sailed for America and arrived in New York, August 20, 1843. They were married in Milwaukee on September 5 of the same year and thereupon walked seventy miles through the wilderness to Lake Koshkonong, where they built their log cabin.

Of this little-known but brilliant naturalist, the distinguished Edward Lee Green, then Professor of Botany at Notre Dame, wrote: "I am confident that, notwithstanding our considerable list of worthy names in American botany, no state has ever had so complete a master of its whole flora as Wisconsin had in this extraordinary man."

Louis Agassiz, for whose Boston museum Kumlien collected many specimens, called him, "the greatest authority in the world on bird nests."

A gull, an aster and an anemone are named in his honor.

1: The Stile Between Two Worlds

page 4 Kumlien, like Thoreau, played the flute, mostly for his own enjoyment but also to lure the birds to answer.

page 8 He corresponded with scientists and curators in museums all over the world. Both Kumlien in his day, and my father some years later, were correspondents of the Smithsonian in Washington, D.C.

page 12 Contemporary experts on *Canis lupus* are almost unanimous in declaring that North American wolves do not voluntarily attack human beings. For many years the Sault Ste. Marie *Daily Star* offered to pay a hundred dollars to anyone who could substantiate an unprovoked attack on man, woman or child. The reward was never collected.

page 12 Every wolf howl differs in some degree from every other wolf howl. It is extremely difficult to notate the wolf's wild wail because it has so many overtones. Lois Crisler in her book *Captive Wild* (New York: Harper and Row, 1968) says of the mourning howl of one of her wolves: "It might rise from D flat to G, return to D flat, and sink away on C. Or go from D up to G flat, come back to D and die on D flat. . . . Always it ended in this 'dying fall,' a semitone lower, like the wail of a grieving woman." Most wolves in my boyhood would answer the lonesome whistle of a railroad engine and today will still answer the warning blast of a Diesel locomotive or the siren of a police car. Some are stimulated to vocalization by the insane laughter of loons.

page 12 Thure Kumlien spoke "pure and classical" English even before he came to America. He read Latin and Greek and corresponded in every modern European language "from Spanish to Swedish."

page 14 Israel Putnam, the hero of the Battle of Bunker Hill, crawled into a wolf den and brought out wolflings when he was a boy. Dr. Adolph Murie, the very distinguished author of *The Wolves of Mt. McKinley,* secured a whelp in a similar manner. George Wilson, who owned several wolves in St. Louis, once crawled down a forty-foot hole leading to the whelping den of one of his "tame" wolves. He carried with him a movie camera and lights and made a remarkable film of the female wolf bringing forth her young. Later one of the small boys of the neighborhood scrambled down the same hole with a flashlight to see the newly born, furry babies.

2: Waiting for Old Three Toes

page 17 The Civil War, which cut off the supply of sugar cane and tobacco grown in the Confederate states, stimulated the planting of tobacco and sugar beets in southern Wisconsin. Edgerton became a thriving market, particularly for tobacco.

page 19   The name of the old, leaky vessel on which Thure, Margretta and her sister Sophia sailed was the *Swea Maria*, a name they later gave to Margretta's daughter. They were ten weeks at sea, and while they were becalmed in mid ocean, the drinking water almost gave out. When the calm was broken, they were nearly shipwrecked in a great storm. Only later did they discover that the sailing ship had been condemned months before they had purchased passage.

page 19   The port of Milwaukee was less than ten years old when Margretta and Thure arrived. It was a rough but thriving frontier village.

page 19   "Lake Koshkonong, when reached by the Kumliens, must fully have answered every expectation of the young naturalist. The lake, some eleven miles long and four in breadth, as I remember it, is but an expansion of Rock River, its sinuous shore line touching the bases of a hundred low hills covered with oaks or overrun with hazel, with many a fair interval of open grassy slope, or widespread lowland meadows. The larger estuaries, sheltered by neighboring groves, their still and shallow waters bordered with green fields of reed and wild rice, were twice in each year the resort of great flocks of wild geese, pelicans, and swans, and indeed of all tribes of waterfowl and wading birds. . . . While the region remained almost unsettled, and while wild birds so abounded, an ornithologist might have been pardoned had he forgotten more or less of his botany. But this one did not. So ardent a lover as he was of all things beautiful in nature, could not but have been enraptured with the floral splendors of wild woodlands and unbroken prairie as they must have appeared to his eye in that early day. . . . Everywhere were to be seen pink and azure banks of phlox and Polemonium, violets, Dentarias and Dielytras, lupines, wild peas, and vetches; extensive yellow beds of Caltha and Ranunculus; meadow patches of scarlet and yellow Castilleias; grassy-leaved Hypoxis, Tradescantia, Camassia, and Zygadenus; hazel borders all undergrown with Erythroniums, Trilliums, Orchis, and nodding wood anemone; thickets of wild rose and shad bush, wild plums and cherries; groves of white-barked aspen and fragrant, rosy-blooming crabapple."

An anonymous botanist quoted by Publius V. Lawson in

The Transactions of the Wisconsin Academy of Sciences, Arts and Letters, Vol. XX.

page 20 Margretta Christine Wallberg was the daughter of a minor officer in the Swedish army, in charge of horses for the King's Cavalry. Thure Kumlien's father, Ludwig Kumlien, like his son to follow, was a graduate of Uppsala. He served for some time in Sweden's Royal Court, and owned and operated several large estates.

page 20 Thure and Margretta worked together in building their cabin. When their little house was finished, Thure wrote to a friend, "It is the nicest log house around here, for we have an extra bedroom besides our one big room. Under the stairs we have a pantry, which is more than most of the pioneers have."

page 23 For a time during the 1840's Thure studied the art of cabinetmaking in a shop in the nearby village of Jefferson. He made Margretta several fine pieces of furniture from the walnut that flourished in their virgin forest.

page 23 The Kumlien children might just as well have purchased a Singer sewing machine, for this brand was also on the market. Many of the present-day industrial firms were already in existence. The early McCormick reapers were the wonder of the fast-growing nation. On these reapers one man drove the team of horses and two men stood on a platform behind him, tying into sheaves the grain that flowed by them. Reaping the grain with a scythe had been a slow and arduous job. Three men and a reaper could cut and bundle ten acres a day.

page 24 Margretta was the graduate of an institution much like our domestic science schools, the highest form of education offered to young women in Sweden in those days. She was not only an expert cook but also helped Thure cut and pile the hay, dig the potatoes and do any and all other forms of farm work. Together they gathered and prepared many wild plants, berries, fruits, nuts, seeds and greens. Thure, being an expert botanist, knew which of the wild mushrooms were safe and savory, and which were poisonous. He believed that, devoid of all other food, they could survive on the "bounty of nature" without the arduous tillage, planting, cultivating and harvesting which consumed so much of their time and energy on their little farm.

page 28   Ellen was being generous to pay seventy-five cents a day for farm labor Although "Civil War inflation" continued after the war until the Panic of 1873, wages were scandalously low. Women in the cities were sweated sixty hours a week for a total of three dollars to five dollars for their six long days of labor. Many hired hands on the farms were paid little more than their keep.

3: The Osprey and the Eagle

page 35   Margarethe Meyer Schurz (1832-1876) and her distinguished husband, Carl Schurz, were a romantic young couple when they arrived in America in 1852. Much has been written about the German-American liberal. It is less well known that his beautiful and highly intelligent wife founded the first kindergarten in America in Watertown, Wisconsin, in 1856. The Schurz home, overlooking Rock River, is approximately twenty-two miles from the village of Busseyville. For more information concerning Mrs. Schurz, see *Margarethe Meyer Schurz*, the delightful, brief biography of Hannah Werwath Swart (Watertown Historical Society, 1967).

page 37   Some raptors which were common in Kumlien's time are rare or extinct in the Koshkonong region today. These include the osprey, the bald eagle, the golden eagle, the gyrfalcon, goshawk and what apparently was Swainson's hawk (now a very rare transient).

Old Abe, the Wisconsin war eagle, was procured in 1861 and served during the Civil War as mascot of the Eagle Regiment, Eighth Wisconsin Infantry. At the sound of the regimental bugle, which he had learned to recognize, he would come to immediate attention. When the cannonading commenced, he would "spread his wings, utter his startling scream" and lead the troops into battle. "The louder the storm, the fiercer and wilder his scream." (*Wisconsin*, American Guide Series. New York: Duell, Sloan and Pearce, 1941.) Greatly loved by the soldiers, he survived thirty-nine battles and skirmishes. After the war he lived until 1881 in a big room fitted for him in the basement of the Wisconsin State Capitol.

page 39   Thure Kumlien began his serious study of ornithology and taxidermy in his early teens. He was literally self taught. Even at Uppsala, which had been the university of his famous predecessor Carl Linnaeus (1707-1778), there was no professor of ornithology in Kumlien's time.

4. Into the Wolf Den

page 44   About four hundred million years ago (according to informed geological estimates) the continent of North America experienced its greatest submersion beneath salt water. Ordovician limestone laid down at about this time shows fossils of trilobites, brachiopods, crinoids and other relatively simple sea creatures.

page 45   The cool draft emerging from the lower entrance of many caves is usually made possible by a higher entrance to the cavern. Cool air falls, presumably sucking in air from above.

page 45   In addition to Israel Putnam, Dr. Adolph Murie and George Wilson, others have crawled into wolf dens. Stanley P. Young and Edward A. Goldman, authors of *The Wolves of North America* (New York, Dover, 1944, 2 volumes) tell of professional wolfers sending their sons into such dens to "drag out young wolves."

page 46   Whooping cranes, now extinct in the region, were fairly common in Kumlien's time. The wild ducks using this branch of the great Mississippi flyway included canvasback, mallards, wood duck, common and red-breasted mergansers, pintails, greater and lesser scaups, blue- and green-winged teal, ruddy ducks, harlequin ducks, oldsquaws, the American widgeon and several other varieties. Until the unfortunate introduction of German carp, which uprooted the beds of wild rice, Koshkonong was one of the greatest "shooting lakes" in North America.

page 46   Wolf hunting has been a favorite "sport" for thousands of years. Several breeds of wolfhounds were developed for this purpose. During the Middle Ages it was often considered the "sport of kings."

page 47   Bats, like wolves, are to some extent the fanciful "creation" of man's lurid imagination. Like all animals, wild and domestic, they sometimes suffer from hydrophobia. The fact that bats fly in the dark, and that a few of the nine hundred varieties are bloodsuckers, combine to horrify some people. Virtually the only chance a bat has to justify his diabolical reputation would occur if one of the South American vampires, who happened to be rabid, should settle upon a victim sleeping in the open.

page 49   Mother wolves do not always carry their young by the loose skin at the nape of the neck. Frequently they pick up the whelp by any portion of the anatomy which is handy, a rear leg for instance. It is a rather shocking sight to see a big-fanged adult put the entire head of one of her puppies into her mouth and carry it—in perfect comfort. Rudyard Kipling, whose wolf lore has often been questioned, was right in saying that a wolf has a mouth so sensitive that it can carry an egg without breaking the shell.

5: Wolf's First Summer

page 57   The great Chicago fire (October 8–10, 1871) destroyed 2,100 acres of buildings worth about two hundred million dollars. Two hundred and fifty people lost their lives. Two-thirds of the city was of frame construction. The summer and early autumn were so excessively dry that the roaring flames, fanned by a high and veering wind, swept away block after block. Thousands of people dashed to the shore of Lake Michigan and waded far out in the water to save themselves from the conflagration. Many Union soldiers, having survived the Civil War, now saw their modest homes go up in smoke. The excessive need for cash and credit to rebuild the city was one of the relatively minor causes of the Panic of 1873.

page 65   The Fourth of July celebration that Robbie missed that year was the tenth anniversary of two Union victories, the capture of Vicksburg and the battle of Gettysburg. Most historians agree that July 4, 1863, was the turning point in the Civil War.

page 70   The Homestead Act of 1862 opened millions of acres of public land to the westward-moving settlers. The requirements for acquiring a quarter section (160 acres) were relatively simple:

The homesteader must be a citizen of the United States or an immigrant in the process of obtaining citizenship; he must be twenty-one years of age; he must pay a fee of fourteen dollars upon filing for the land; he must stake out his acreage, build a house or cabin and make certain improvements; he must cultivate part of the land; and finally, he must live on the land for five years.

After 1872 it was much easier for a Civil War veteran to acquire such a homestead. He could apply his years in the army to the five-year requirement.

6: Thirteenth Birthday

page 73 Field mice (Microtus) are the most numerous mammals in North America. These mice (or voles), of which there are about fifty species, begin to breed at the age of three weeks. In one famous laboratory experiment it was discovered that under optimum conditions a female mouse may bear seventeen litters a year, while her first daughter has time to bear thirteen litters. Were it not for owls, hawks, cats, weasels, wolves, coyotes and other "predators," the mouse population would swiftly and literally cover the earth. A population explosion of meadow mice occurred in the Humboldt Valley of Nevada in 1907. They soon devoured all the grainfields, gardens and alfalfa above the ground, and every edible root beneath the ground. "Within two years, when the peak was reached, it was estimated that on many large ranches there were from five to eight million mice to each square mile." See Eugene Burns, *The Sex Life of Wild Animals* (New York: Rinehart & Co., 1953).

page 74 On Isle Royale in Lake Superior a long-time study of the wolf and moose populations has been made by L. David Mech, Ph.D., and others. Since all wildlife on this island is completely protected from man, this has become the perfect place to investigate the relationship between the shaggy "predators" and the big ungulates. To oversimplify a bit, the wolves perform the very necessary service of keeping the moose herd at about a thousand or under. Above that figure the moose endanger their food supply and begin to die of disease and starvation. These wolves apparently are able to restrict their own population, keeping their number to between nineteen and twenty-seven individuals.

page 74 Kumlien apparently foresaw the danger to the billions of passenger pigeons. He left beautifully mounted examples of this species to the University of Wisconsin, Whitewater Normal School (now a university) and other schools of higher learning. The last passenger pigeon on earth died in a Cincinnati zoo in 1914.

page 75 Kumlien had made a watercolor of his birthplace (Hertrop, Härlunda parish, Sweden). It hung in the cabin as a constant and nostalgic reminder of his boyhood. Like his father and his father's father, he was an amateur artist of some skill. It is, therefore, not surprising that his youngest offspring not only painted, but also drew plans for the new house.

page 85 The speed at which wolves react is phenomenal. George Wilson, who has raised, bred, filmed and studied a number of wolves, had one wolf that liked to eat cigarettes. While filming a sequence of this wolf, the animal snatched a cigarette from the lips of one of Wilson's companions. The action was so lightning swift that it had not registered on the movie film. By carefully calculating the infinitesimal lapse between frames of the high-speed camera, Wilson discovered that the theft had been accomplished in one-thirtieth of a second.

7: The Panic of 1873

page 88 For a more complete summary of the causes of the Panic of 1873, please see Allan Nevins, *The Emergence of Modern America, 1865–1878.* (New York: Macmillan, 1927).

page 90 In the summer of 1866, the *Nation* proclaimed, "Of all the epidemics that have swept over our land, the swiftest and most infectious is croquet." Allan Nevins adds, "Every lawn from the Atlantic to the Mississippi seemed to have been impressed into service. Expensive English sets of balls and mallets found a large sale." The game has survived until the present day.

page 92 John Rogers created realistic statuary groups, which were then cast in great numbers. Most of these reproductions sold at prices ranging from fifteen to twenty-five dollars. "Rarest of the Rogers groups are the salesmen's samples in miniature, of a size less than 4 inches high." See Carl W. Drepperd, *A Dictionary of American Antiques* (New York: Doubleday & Co., 1952).

8: Wolf Goes to School

page 93 The Tweed ring was probably the most corrupt gang of politicians which ever mismanaged the city of New York. An evil alliance between the metropolitan Democrats, ruled by "Boss" Tweed, and the upstate Republicans, made it possible to misappropriate an estimated 85 percent of the city's income. Tweed became a multimillionaire almost overnight. He was finally sentenced to prison and died in jail. But it was said that the twenty million dollars that he and his friends had stolen could have made New York the most beautiful city in the world.

page 97 "Wolves, unlike dogs, are never wishy-washy." This very perceptive analysis was made by Elizabeth Ashby, who with her photographer husband, Sullivan Ashby, owns several wolves, wolf-dogs and coyotes. We are fortunate in having them for neighbors, since it has allowed frequent observation of their moody but affectionate pack.

page 97 Little Red Ridinghood, a fairy tale by the well-named Brothers Grimm, has probably poisoned more minds against wolves than any other fable in print. It has been virtually impossible to discover an authenticated and documented instance of a wolf killing a man, woman or child in modern times. Several explanations have been suggested. Very few wolves are rabid. But it is quite conceivable that a rabid wolf, like a rabid dog, might (in his diseased insanity) attack a human being. As previously stated, there may be a difference in the aggressive tendencies of European and American wolves. It is also possible that wolves, before the invention of guns, had less respect for Homo sapiens than they have today. There is no doubt, however, that wolves have killed many domestic animals, particularly where man has destroyed the wild creatures which previously provided their larder. Wolves apparently do not kill for the sheer joy of slaughter. Carcasses are usually well devoured, and what may be left helps to feed a dozen lesser "predators" and "scavengers"—both words being more emotional than descriptive.

page 97 Coyotes, like young wolves, often devour grasshoppers, literally by the thousands. The examinations of many stomachs have shown instances in which 50 percent or more of the contents consisted of grasshoppers. This diet, of course, is merely temporary summer fare.

9: The Parlor Organ

page 100 The author has eaten muskrat meat, which provides a stew as palatable as that made from squirrel or rabbit. For many years muskrat carcasses were labeled "marsh rabbits" and were shipped to the cities in barrels.

page 104 More than one hundred American manufacturers of nineteenth-century pianos and organs are listed by Carl W. Drepperd in *A Dictionary of American Antiques* (New York: Doubleday & Co., 1952). Several of these firms are still doing a brisk business.

page 106 Counterpanes were made by two major methods.

They were hand woven, or they were quilted from carefully scissored bits of wool, silk or cotton minutely stitched together. They were called by many names, sometimes Biblical, poetic or merely whimsical. Star of the East, Chips and Whetstones and Tennessee Lace are a few that come to mind.

page 107 Perhaps it was "shyness" or perhaps "Victorian prudery," but among white, middle-class husbands and wives few kisses were openly observed. Mark Twain relates that his boyhood town, Hannibal, Missouri, was not a "kissing community." His father shook hands with his wife and children before they all went to bed. As his father lay dying, with the family gathered around him, he called only his daughter Pamela to him, kissed her and then died.

page 108 Although later discoveries and experiments have superseded much of the scientific information in *A School Compendium of Natural and Experimental Philosophy,* by Richard Green Parker, A.M., it remains an exciting and important textbook. First published in the year 1837, it filled the need for a simple, nontechnical introduction to virtually all the sciences of that day. Revised again and again to keep up with "the exact sciences," it intrigued the minds of many young people, including Thomas Edison, who read it from cover to cover and attempted most of the experiments.

page 109 The poetic proclamation that a wolf can "hear a cloud passing over" should be credited to George Wilson, who has raised, observed and photographed many wolves. As a more specific example, he tells of one of his wolves who could hear the almost inaudible whisper of a mercury switch.

page 110 For the remarkable variations in "wolf music" and their individualized responses, please see Russell J. Rutter and Douglas H. Pimlott, *The World of the Wolf* (Philadelphia: J. B. Lippincott Co., 1968).

page 111 "Such [freight] rates meant that when corn was seventy cents a bushel in the East it might be fifteen cents in the local market in Iowa or central Illinois." Please see Allan Nevins, *The Emergence of Modern America,* page 163. The railroads at that time were so powerful and often so corrupt that they were able to bribe state legislatures to avoid any regulation of their rates. Also, by secret rebates, they could rule or ruin any industry.

page 111 The farmers were understandably angered by the

stranglehold of the railroads, and the atrocious interest rates, often rising to 15 and even 20 percent, which they paid on their mortgages. These independent agriculturalists, who have always been noteworthy as nonjoiners, *did,* however, join the Grange. Founded in 1868 by two organizers with no funds whatsoever, it grew so rapidly that by the spring of 1874 it had 1,500,000 members. Grange sentiment made a large impact upon law-making bodies. Without the approval of these "embattled farmers," the average state assemblyman had no chance of being elected. Freight rates were regulated, interest rates slowly subsided and farm machinery manufacturers cut their prices amazingly. In the meantime, the panic had caused thousands of foreclosures and bankruptcies. Many poverty-stricken farm families packed their shabby belongings into a farm wagon and started west.

10: The Shanty Boat

page 116 For a century and three-quarters, St. Louis has played a dominant role in the fur trade. Documents in Spanish, French and English reveal a lively commerce there in pelts of beaver, otter, mink, fox, bear and virtually all other fur-bearing animals of the upper Mississippi and Missouri valleys. It was from a camp near St. Louis that Lewis and Clark launched their historic journey of exploration across the continent. It was from St. Louis that many of the Mountain Men set forth with their upriver cargoes of trade goods for the Indians. Beavers were nearly exterminated by the trappers. They were saved by the coincidence that beaver hats went out of style in the late 1830's, thus drastically reducing the value of the skins.

page 117 For decades the price paid for wolfskins was approximately $1.50. They were not considered a fine fur by the dealers, who, however, could sell them in great quantities to the Russian army, whose soldiers were clothed in wolfskin coats to protect them from bitter winter weather. Wolves can safely sleep in the open in fifty degrees below zero temperature.

11: The Wolf at the Door

page 121 Wolves in the wild follow a hunting trail which roughly defines their territory. In summer this may be an area of modest proportions near the den. In winter these trails may curve out and back for one hundred miles. Even at maximum density, it takes about ten square miles of wilderness to feed each wolf.

page 123 Buffalo robes were common in all the colder regions of the United States. Millions of buffalo were slain for "sport." Often the hunter took only the tongue and the hide.

12: The Race Is to the Swift

page 128 Lois Crisler, in her excellent *Arctic Wild* (New York: Harper and Row, 1958) tells how difficult it is for a wolf to overtake a caribou. Even at three weeks of age, these swift, long-legged animals can outdistance their pursuers. Usually wolves make many attempts, but give up quickly when they find themselves outpaced. If an old or sickly animal falls behind, he swiftly becomes the prey of *Canis lupus*.

page 129 For more about the Morgan breed, please see Ralph Moody's delightful and dependable volume *American Horses* (Boston: Houghton Mifflin Company, 1962).

13: The House-Raising

page 134 Oak is heavier than water. Some of these massive hewn-oak beams weighed as much as one hundred pounds to the linear foot. The author of this book, who built a cabin of such beams on the Rock River near Indian Ford, can testify to the labor involved. Please see Sterling North, *Hurry Spring!* (New York: E. P. Dutton, 1966).

page 138 The author also played the five-string banjo at country dances a little more than half a century ago. During a dance one New Year's Eve, in Fulton, Wisconsin, one of the sturdy male dancers literally "swung" his partner. Her feet left the floor so near to our little orchestra that the heel of her shoe pierced the head of my banjo.

page 140 Margretta Christine Kumlien died on September 22, 1874. Her granddaughter, Angie Kumlien Main, gives the date of Thure Kumlien's death as August 5, 1888. So Thure outlived his beloved wife by nearly fourteen years. Their bodies lie side by side in Sweet's Cemetery near Albion, Wisconsin. See *Wisconsin Magazine of History*, Vol. 27, No. 3 (March, 1944).

14: A Boy's Will Is the Wind's Will

page 144 Kumlien's spring was still running cold and clear the last time I visited his eighty-acre farm. The spring was surrounded by a bed of mint that the old naturalist had planted himself. "Water always tastes colder and sweeter if you first nibble a leaf of mint." David Willard North in a letter to his son Sterling, November, 1942.

15: Preparation for the Big Event

page 151   *Nelumbo lutea,* the American lotus, still bloomed in lavish abundance upon this little lake a few years ago. But the water table has been falling in the area for several decades. This may eventually doom these beautiful big floating flowers.

page 154   Tobacco, sometimes called "Green Gold" by its raisers, is the most profitable crop, acre for acre, in southern Wisconsin. It is also the most laborious.

16: The Fourth of July

page 158   "Now I've seen the elephant" was one of the catch phrases of the era. It apparently meant, "Now I've seen everything."

page 158   There were several such cycloramas painted at about this time. One showed the Mississippi River from source to mouth.

page 159   The Sells Brothers began their circus in 1872. The Ringling Brothers, based in nearby Baraboo, Wisconsin, opened in 1882. But the circus in one form or another had been popular since Roman times. It was a well-known form of entertainment in England before the first English emigrants ventured across the Atlantic. Small traveling circuses were common in nineteenth-century America.

page 160   As mentioned, the Grange did indeed force state legislatures to lower freight rates. They also founded firms to manufacture farm implements at far lower prices. Readers may be surprised to learn that Montgomery Ward was started at this time as an agency of the Grange. Their first catalogue was a single sheet of printed paper.

Grateful acknowledgment is hereby given—

To Art and Carrie Cunningham who searched out and photographed the graves of Thure and Margretta Christine Kumlien in Sweet's old cemetery near Albion, Wisconsin.

To Royal and Beulah Ladd, who found and photostated early plats of the Koshkonong region.

To Hannah Werwath Swart, who furnished needed copies of the *Wisconsin Magazine of History*.

To Eleanor Wild, who has typed the manuscripts of my ten most recent books.

And finally, to my incredibly patient and loving wife Gladys, who for the last forty-two years has been my helpmeet and companion. Few indeed in this world have asked so little and given so much.

READ YOUR WAY TO ADVENTURE

And share the joys and frustrations, triumphs and
defeats of other young people.

☐ 2459	**BAD FALL** by Charles P. Crawford In this chilling tale of evil, a shy boy's friendship with a strange newcomer turns into a terrifying nightmare.	95¢
☐ 12347	**SUMMER OF MY GERMAN SOLDIER** by Bette Greene A lonely Jewish girl forms a tragic friendship with a runaway prisoner of war.	$1.75
☐ 12587	**THE WOLFLING** by Sterling North Life of a growing boy and his wolf-cub pet on a frontier farm.	$1.75
☐ 10691	**DOWN THE LONG HILLS** by Louis L'Amour Can a young boy and girl stranded all alone survive starvation, Indian raids, savage outlaws, and wild animals?	$1.50
☐ 11992	**STAR TREK 10** by James Blish Spock views the forbidden Kollos and goes insane—and much more—in 6 new episodes from the TV series.	$1.75
☐ 11288	**WHERE THE RED FERN GROWS** by Wilson Rawls Billy loves his coon hounds and trains them to be champions, but tragedy lies ahead.	$1.50

Buy them at your local bookstore or use this handy coupon for ordering: